HOTSHOT

a Dugan Heywood mystery

David W. Barber

Since by Man came Death…
A small town shares its secrets.

INDENT PUBLISHING

IndentPublishing.com

HOTSHOT

Print edition first published in Canada in 2025
ebook edition published 2025
No AI was used in the writing or production of this book

Cover design by McNeill Design Arts

Indent Publishing
IndentPublishing.com
contact@IndentPublishing.com

Canadian Cataloguing in Publication Data

Barber, David W. (David William)
HOTSHOT

ISBN 978-1-998904-21-1

Cataloguing data available from Library and Archives Canada

Author's Note

Welcome to *Hotshot*, my third Dugan Heywood mystery, where once again readers will find themselves in the (fictional) staid old university town of Grayston. And once again ex-journalist turned church musician Dugan finds himself with a deadly puzzle to solve.

I'm grateful to readers of *Hedshot* (Indent Publishing, 2023) and *Mugshot* (Indent Publishing, 2024), my previous two Dugan Heywood mysteries, who enjoyed them enough to ask that I continue Dugan's story. I hope you'll find this one equally engaging.

My thanks to Jacques Lauzon and Indent Publishing for their continued work and support of our publishing ventures. And for this novel in particular, my thanks to friends and early readers Paddy, Janice, Jan, Mary Anne and Julie (who also designed the lovely cover) for their careful attention and helpful suggestions. And to Brett for sparking a central idea.

– DWB
Toronto, 2025

Chapter 1

The proud have imagined a lie against me,
but I will keep thy precepts with my whole heart.

– Psalm 119, v. 69

I guess I'm a professional musician now. And no longer a journalist.

My friend Bill Garner was officially retired. Diabetes had made his life difficult. Dimmed his eyesight, taken his right foot and part of that leg. Losing most of his sight, Bill said, made teaching a challenge not worth confronting on a daily basis. And losing the leg made playing the church organ difficult. Effectively impossible.

So both his professions – teacher full time and musician part time – had become too much of a burden to bear. So, as he said – with typical self-effacing dark humor from someone with only one leg – it was time for him to "take a step back."

Which is where I came in.

Bill was – had been – a professor of English literature at the university in Grayston, a small, staid old university town on the shores of a big old and sometimes less staid lake.

As well as being an English prof, Bill had also had a side gig as music director/organist at St. Quentin's, a small Episcopalian church located, conveniently for him, just a few blocks off campus. Within walking distance – at least when he could still walk – of both his office and his home.

Nearly three years ago – time flies – Bill had taken a research sabbatical and I'd taken a temp gig as his replacement at the church. There were plenty of grad students eager to pick up his academic burden but fewer qualified to take on his musical duties. The sabbatical was supposed to be just a year. But Bill's health had worsened, landing him in hospital.

So the church committee in charge of such things had extended my contract indefinitely, assuming (hoping – praying, as they are inclined to do) that Bill would soon return to reclaim the organ bench. Most had seemed happy enough with me in the meantime, though I'll readily admit Bill was a better musician than I. A better organist, for sure.

But with Bill gone, the committee – and who knows what other forces in the byzantine world of church politics – would at some point begin looking for a fulltime replacement. I was pretty sure I'd be in contention for the job. At least I hoped so. But there were no guarantees.

I was born into a long line of Unitarians, but I'd long since lapsed from even that minimal structure. (Can you be any more lapsed than a lapsed Unitarian? Hard to imagine.)

There's still some debate on many sides whether Unitarians should even be considered Christian. Opinion remains divided. For my part, I say no. Seems a contradiction in terms. The clue's right in the name. Unitarian, not trinitarian – which seems kind of the foundational principle. But because of a decent singing voice, as a small boy I was abducted by Anglicans. So I'd grown up trapped in the trappings and fine music of a traditional Anglican (in my case Episcopalian) men-and-boys choir. Steeped like the finest tea in the music of Byrd, Tallis, Tomkins and the rest. Purcell. S. Wesley, his 'natural son' S.S. Wesley, Attwood and Walmisley. Stanford in G. Stanford in B-flat, Sumsion in G. The organ swell and grandeur of H. Balfour Gardiner's *Te lucis ante terminum*. The lush simplicity of

Stanford's *Beati quorum.* A bit more recently, Howells, RVW, Kelly in C and even (God help us) Rutter.

Fake it til you make it, the old saying goes. When it comes to church music, I don't just fake it, I know my stuff. And I love it sincerely. In most quarters I daresay I even know theology and can argue exegesis with the best of them. Hell, I've even read *De trinitatis erroribus* (*On the Errors of the Trinity*), a treatise by 16th-century Spanish doctor, philosopher and theologian Michael Servetus, the work that got him burned at the stake as a heretic, his books tied around his waist. The closest thing Unitarians have to a patron saint.

And I know the Bible pretty well, especially the psalms from singing them all the time, can often quote you chapter and verse – even though I barely believe a word of it. Except the general principal of love your neighbor as yourself. Which seems like good advice regardless of whoever may have said it.

But it's not like I wear my godlessness on my sleeve. Bill knew. He'd been pretty much in the same boat himself, though he was more poetic about it. The minister knows and doesn't mind. His job is to forgive me anyway. He's in the forgiveness business. I'd bet most of the congregation thinks I fit right in, was safely just another sheep in the fold.

But you know how gossip is. Someone picks up a tiny shred of it, a thread of it, and starts pulling. I guess it gives them a feeling of power. Small power for small minds. And some of those small minds had a mind to find themselves a properly churchy church musician.

I know Hugh Parry, the minister, is in my corner. He and I have an easygoing relationship, for which I'm grateful. I know from long experience singing in church choirs and generally hanging around in that abstruse world that heads of ministry and of music do not always get along. Quite often clash. Butt heads, as it were. So I was glad for Hugh's support.

But I know a few others in the congregation and among its various committees and subcommittees and exploratory task forces sometimes whisper behind their hands. And not always behind my back. Those few feel it unseemly – nay, perhaps even ungodly – that the church should have in its midst an agnostic like me. (They cannot, of course, discern the subtle but crucial difference between an agnostic and an atheist. So they tar me with that brush.) And worse, in their mind, I'm not just a congregant but the music director. At least *pro tem*. But not for much longer if they have any say in the matter, believe you me.

So my future at St. Quentin's was suddenly in some doubt.

Chapter 2

Deliver me not over into the will of mine adversaries,
for there are false witnesses risen up against me,
and such as speak wrong.

– Ps. 27, v. 14

That's OK. I was used to it.

Before taking on my church gig, for about two decades I'd been a professional journalist. At various times a reporter, copy editor or editor at the *Grayston Gazette*. In its glory years it had been a small but respectable independent newspaper serving the small city and its surrounding region. I was proudly an ink-stained wretch in a noble, though hardly lucrative, profession. But the dead-tree industry had been slowly dying even as I came on board. The advent of the internet had ramped up its decline, stealing away news and advertising (especially classified ads) even more than radio and then TV had already been doing.

So as a struggling independent, and despite the efforts of its supportive owner/publisher, the paper and its staff had suffered many years of belt-tightening, then a hiring freeze, then more budget cutbacks and staff cuts by attrition. We were used to having the sword – or rather ax – of Damocles hanging over our heads.

The final blow for me and for many came when Blackwell – Blackwell Holdings Inc, a giant, faceless conglomerate – added that small paper to its ever-growing portfolio and began a heartless round of drastic "restructuring."

In other words, layoffs. Even a few firings. For cause, if Blackwell could find or manufacture an excuse not to have to pay a proper severance.

Which is how I'd found myself an ex-journalist who was now a church musician. Dismissed without cause, at least I'd managed to squeeze a severance out of them. For that, I counted myself lucky.

Meantime, the dregs of that severance and the church gig were keeping a roof over my head and kibble in my dog's bowl.

On rare occasions, church committees can loose the fateful lightning of a terrible swift sword, can render a decision quickly and with ruthless efficiency.

But most times, I know, they move at a pace that would make a sloth envious.

So I figured my job and I were safe for now. And for a while yet to come.

No time to think about that. I was too busy actually doing the job.

So at the moment I was sitting at the battered old Steinway grand in the church hall looking over the music for tonight's rehearsal. The piano is old, battle-scarred and slightly out of tune but still a reliable workhorse, donated many decades ago by a grateful parishioner and just as gratefully received by whoever was Bill's predecessor at the time.

My cellphone made its text message sound. I've been playing around with these. Right now it's the "*dun-dun*" from *Law & Order*.

It was one of my sopranos, a high school girl named Lucy, asking if she could leave practice early. She had an essay to finish.

I resisted the urge to text back that she had some 'splaining to do. She was far too young to get the reference. And it would only remind me how old I already feel.

I remembered my high school days from – ahem – a few years ago. For most of us the first time in our lives we experience actual workloads and real deadlines. And performance pressure. It's why – even well into our adult lives – we're sometimes still haunted by those dreams of the big exam we forgot to study for.

I figured Lucy had enough on her plate without me teasing her. So I texted back. Yes, she could leave early. Stay long enough to run through Sunday's music, then she could bail.

"*Dun-dun.*"

Lucy texted back: "*Thx! cu 2nite*"

If only all our problems were so easily solved.

On top of the regular grind of weekly choir rehearsals and Sunday services – a church music director's life is circumscribed by Thursday evenings and Sunday mornings – I was rehearsing the choir for a big concert to come in May. And, as (bad) luck would have it, the concert date was set for a Saturday that this year happens to come not long after Easter – since Easter has this annoying habit of moving around the calendar. And that, liturgically and musically, is already a busy time of year.

So in terms of our workload, April was indeed going to be the cruelest month. Thanks a lot, T. S. Eliot.

Whose bright idea had that been? I had only myself to blame. That and a whole set of circumstances beyond my control. Well, if I've learned anything from my years of kayaking, when the water gets rough, you've just got to go with the flow.

We had a few months to go before the big concert. And we'd already begun rehearsing not long after we'd polished off Christmas and all its musical demands. So for now we were sticking to our regular Thursday/Sunday routine. I'd been stealing some time from Thursday's rehearsals of the Sunday music to get ahead on the concert music. No need yet for extra rehearsals. As we got closer to the gig, I might have to ask my singers to come a bit early or stay late, or even give up a Saturday morning or two. Depending on how we progressed.

So far, I was pleased with their work and feeling optimistic about the final result.

I should have known better than to tempt Fate.

Chapter 3

O praise the Lord with me
and let us magnify his name together.

– Ps. 34, v. 3

We were gearing up to perform Handel's beloved oratorio *Messiah*. It will be a first for my choir. We'd done a few bits for a Christmas concert before. But never the whole thing. Some of the singers already know it well, having sung it elsewhere over the years. It's standard repertoire. And lots of others in the choir have heard it, in concert and/or on recordings, even if they've never actually sung it. So they're at least familiar with it.

Which is both a benefit and a problem, as it turns out. And as I was beginning to discover.

Messiah is so well known, in fact such an old warhorse, that some singers think they know it upside down and backwards. And they know it so well that they think they don't need to rehearse. Or at least rehearse so much. I've already had requests from a few who want to skip most of the practice time until we get closer.

"C'mon, Dugan," one of the tenors had said to me, "Lemme just come back for the dress and the gig. You know I'm good for it."

In his case, I knew he probably was. But I worried about setting a dangerous precedent. Besides, it's not just about knowing the notes. It's also about being able to blend in and sing well together with the others in the choir. And to work well with the conductor.

That would be me.

So I asked that singer instead to come to as many rehearsals as he could manage and skip or leave early for as few as possible. Others, like Lucy, had a legitimate reason to leave early once in a while. And we were still in early days. I was glad she'd asked permission first. Others just missed practice without notice and seemed to go on the old assumption that forgiveness is easier to obtain than permission. Which, I have to admit, is usually true.

The tenor was Jordan Baxter, my section lead, who would be our tenor soloist for the gig. He'd be joining in with the rest of the section for some of the choruses, as long as it didn't hamper his solo work. They'd appreciate his help. The tenor soloist makes a big splash at the opening with *Comfort Ye* and *Ev'ry valley*. But depending on which movements you sing and which you drop – there are too many movements, and too many versions of them, to do them all – he might not have a whole lot to do on his own after that.

My choir of St. Quentin's was joining forces with the choir of St. Andrew's Presbyterian in Alliston, a town smaller than Grayston about 30 miles away. I'd met their music director, Christine Tanaka, at an ecumenical event for church music directors last summer. We'd hit it off, musically speaking, and when she suggested this joint concert, I thought it might be fun.

Many in my choir had been bugging me to do *Messiah* ever since I took the job. But it's a big deal, demanding of both time and money. And musical effort. So sharing the workload, costs and musical resources with another choir seemed like a good idea. Make the yoke easier and the burthen lighter, as it were.

But still, joining together two choirs – who'd been

rehearsing with two different directors who I'm sure, despite their musical compatibility, have different styles and approaches – was going to be a challenge. Christine and I had already talked a lot about how we wanted it to sound. And more or less we were on the same page. But there were still issues for us to work out and solve with the choirs.

Chapter 4

O clap your hands together, all ye peoples;
O sing unto God with the voice of melody.

– Ps. 47, v. 1

One other factor had fallen into place to make this project possible. For many decades, any performance of *Messiah* in Grayston had been the sole property of St. Nicholas, the much larger, better funded and (in its own mind) far more important Episcopalian church in town.

This was especially true during the long tenure of its imperious former music director, Julian Gascoyne. Gascoyne's grip on St. Nick's, and so his hold on the musical life of the town – or at least on many of its richest and most important families – was ironclad and in some ways ruthless. Even before Gascoyne, *Messiah* at St. Nicholas had long been an annual Christmas tradition. Gascoyne had just cemented that certainty by force of will. And I imagine a considerable amount of personal coercion.

But a devastating scandal, a moral lapse of staggering proportions, had seen Gascoyne revealed as a sexual predator and sent off to prison. When I was still at the paper, I'd played a small role in helping investigate and uncover the truth of that terrible story. Then later, after I'd left the paper and moved to my church gig, I'd also helped uncover another facet of the scandal that had left so many hurt and wounded people in its wake.

Among those most sadly missed was Priya Patel, a lovely and talented soprano in my choir and briefly a girlfriend of mine. We'd parted but remained friends. Then later she'd died – been murdered, in fact. And I'd found myself, without expecting to, helping the police and my old colleagues at the *Gazette* to uncover her killer.

And then, because the stain of those events seemed like it might never go away, I'd ended up being caught up in another murder too. It was getting to be a habit I hoped would never repeat itself. After all, how many murders can an ex-journalist turned church musician be expected to solve? Especially in a small town.

Whether to distance himself from the cloud of Gascoyne, or maybe just because he was tired of it, the new music director at St. Nick's, Matthew Court, had decided not to perform *Messiah* this season. He chose instead to have a concert of Bach's *Christmas Oratorio* – three of the six cantatas that make up the whole work. I'd gone to hear it in December and he'd done a fine job. In a spirit of generosity, Matthew had also agreed to share the wealth. So St. Nick's, St. Quentin's and several other churches in Grayston and the surrounding region had agreed to form a little music committee by which we agreed to take turns performing *Messiah* in different places over the next few years.

In the choral world, *Messiah* is not just an old warhorse. It's also a cash cow. Audiences love it. Never seem to tire of hearing it year after year. Hence the long (and lucrative) run of the St. Nick's monopoly. Like many singers, many orchestral players have come to know it well. So you can usually find players and throw together a pickup band without much trouble and – for the instruments, anyway – on only a few rehearsals. Thus cutting down on costs. Other than the soloists, most singers aren't paid, whereas the instrumentalists expect to be. Fair enough. They can usually come and do it on two rehearsals. But other than ringers who might parachute in, like my tenor Jordan, not as many singers can do that.

That's how you sometimes get the slightly unflattering, divisive label of 'singers' as distinct from 'musicians.' As if one group doesn't include the other. Singers tend to bristle at that one. Mostly it's done in jest. Mostly.

Among the advantages of teaming up with Christine and St. Andrew's, aside from sharing costs and combining our choral forces into a choir of decent size, is that between us we had a full complement of soloists. Almost. Priya was my star (in more ways than one). But with her gone, I didn't have a soprano of her calibre. Oh, I have a pretty decent soprano section lead who works hard and sings well. But she has a small voice and a tendency to stage fright. She was actually relieved to learn that Christine has a strong soprano in her choir to carry those solos. Christine also has a solid bass. Which is more than I have. So she was providing him too.

Which left me to fill the inner voices. I have a terrific tenor in Jordan to add to the solo mix. But that still left us to find an alto soloist. I have a contralto lead in my section who's musically dependable, but alas less so when it comes to scheduling. Her work demands often take her away at unpredictable times and at the last minute. Under the circumstances, she'd asked for everyone's sake that we find someone else.

Christine, for her part, has several women in her alto section. One who was maybe a solid contender if she decided to audition and a few others who – though welcome enough for a normal Sunday church service – were, we had to admit, past their prime as soloists. On the other end of the spectrum, Christine has one promising young contralto coming up in the ranks. She's keen and eager. But she's musically inexperienced and both she and her voice are young, untrained and still yet too small. The alto solos in *Messiah* are musically and emotionally demanding and both Christine and I felt this young woman, still in her teens, wasn't quite ready for them. Give her a few more years and she might wow the crowd.

But for now that left us one alto soloist short.

Chapter 5

If the Lord had not helped me,
my soul would soon have dwelt in silence.

– Ps. 94, v. 17

That was a worry for another day. I was foolishly hopeful that someone would turn up. Matthew at St. Nick's might have one. And there were a few other choirs around who might provide one if we asked. I'd already put the word out among most of the other choral directors I know or know of in the wider area, hoping they might be able to help.

Someone was bound to cough up a good alto. You should pardon the expression.

Choir practice went well. We'd passed Ash Wednesday – and that wonderful church tradition of the night before, the Pancake Tuesday supper – and were into the sombre season of Lent, the 40-some days leading up to Easter. (Judging from their bad grammar, some people would probably call it 'loaned.')

Unless you were going to tackle the challenge of the gorgeous Allegri *Miserere*, with its parade of soprano high notes soaring above the rest of the choir below – and we weren't ready for that – Lenten music tends by its nature to be simple and unadorned. The church term is ferial, from the Latin for an ordinary weekday. And which some choir members (I blush to include myself) sometimes jokingly call 'feral,' as in a wild animal. We like to keep ourselves amused.

But that meant more time we could devote to rehearsing *Messiah* – which was one of several good reasons to be doing it in spring and not Christmas, when most people do it. There are other reasons too.

"OK, that's a wrap," I said to my singers at the end of practice. "It's coming along nicely. Thanks for all your hard work."

It was true. But I also know you catch more flies with honey.

"Oh, and by the way," I said, "since Meg –" I looked over and gave a friendly nod to our alto section lead "– will be too busy with her crazy workload to be our alto soloist, we still need to find one for the performance. If anyone here wants to audition, please let me know. And if anyone knows someone among your singer friends who might also like to audition, do please ask around and let me know too.

"That's it," I said. "See you at the usual time, 9:30 Sunday morning. Don't party too much on Saturday night."

That last bit was more of a tiny joke than anything. There weren't many heavy partyers in my choir. Most of them were either too young to drink, too old to bother going out or just too tired from working all week.

Choir members began putting their music away in their cubbyholes and helpfully stacking the curved-wood-and-metal chairs along one of the walls of Macmillan Hall, the church hall where we practice, next door to the church itself. They were chatting easily among themselves and putting on their coats. We hadn't had much snow lately, but the February weather was its usual dreary and cold.

As I was closing the piano lid and putting on the dark blue fitted cover to protect the finish, one of my sopranos came up looking like she wanted to speak with me.

"Mr. Heywood. Dugan?" she said. Her name is Marcie

Harding, She's in her first year – or maybe second? I lose track – at the university. Making her not much older than Lucy Neville, who had indeed ducked out early to work on her paper.

"Hi, Marcie," I said. "What's up?"

"I might know of an alto soloist for you," she said.

"Really?" I said. "Who is it?"

"My boyfriend's a countertenor," she said. "And I know he's sung *Messiah* a few times before, both in the chorus and as a soloist. But he's travelling right now and I'm not sure what his timing will be in May. If it's OK with you, I can ask him if he's interested and available."

A countertenor? That would be great, I thought to myself. If he's any good.

Marcie has been in my choir only since the start of the season in September, so I haven't had a chance to get to know her very well. But she's never struck me as someone who's prone to exaggeration or seeking special attention. Still, call me cynical, but "my boyfriend is a countertenor" might have a tinge of that old joke about the film director casting his latest movie and the producer saying, "my girlfriend's an actress…"

"Well, do ask him," I said, cautiously polite. "And if the timing works out, maybe we can set up an audition."

No point overcommitting myself until I've heard him sing.

"Sure," Marcie said. "Grayston is supposed to call me tonight from the road anyway. So I'll be sure to ask him."

That stopped me for a moment.

"Your boyfriend's name is Grayston?"

"I know, right?" she said. "Same as the city I live in.

Ironic. Everyone ribs me about it. And it makes for confusing conversations sometimes."

"No," I said, to clarify. "Your boyfriend is a countertenor?"

"Yes."

"And his name is Grayston?"

"Ye-e-e-s?" Marcie said tentatively. Not sure what I was driving at.

"Not," I said, "Grayston Bergdorf?"

"Yes," she smiled, relieved. "That's him!"

"Your boyfriend is Grayston Bergdorf," I said. "One of the most promising young countertenors on the music scene today?"

"Yup!" she smiled. Proudly this time. "His career *has* been taking off lately. He's on a concert tour right now. Awful time of year to be on the road. And I hate that it keeps us apart so much. But he does what his agent tells him to. You know how it is."

I guess I do. But not at his level.

"So should I ask him?" Marcie said.

"Well, hell, Marcie," I said, trying not to sound too giddy. "If Grayston Bergdorf is available and willing to sing for us, he can have the job. No question. Done deal. I'd be honored to hire him. If we can afford him. Tell him he doesn't even have to audition. Just promise to show up for the dress rehearsal and the gig."

"That's really nice," she said. As if *I* were the one doing *her* a favor. "I'll tell him. I really hope he can do it."

"Not to be too demanding," I said, "but if he has time, it would great to meet with him at least once before the dress so we can go over tempos and phrasing and whatever he has in mind for ornaments and cadenzas. If he's busy, we could probably do that by phone if that works for him. No big deal."

"Thanks, Mr. Heywood," Marcie said. "I'd better be going. I'm hoping he'll call soon. I'll let you know what he says."

"Thanks."

Grayston Bergdorf as our alto soloist for *Messiah*. Wow.

We were going to have ourselves an honest-to-God hotshot.

Chapter 6

A freewill offering will I give to thee
and praise thy Name, O Lord,
because it is so comfortable.

– Ps. 54, v. 6

A couple of days passed. Saturday early afternoon I got a call.

"Hi, Mr. Heywood. It's Marcie Harding."

"Hi, Marcie. What's up?"

"I spoke with my boyfriend," she said. "He says he'd be happy to be our alto soloist for *Messiah*. He had to juggle a few things, but he was able to do that. So now he's available for us."

Be still, my heart.

"That's terrific news, Marcie," I said, trying to remain cool and professional. As if having a world-class soloist in our little town was no big deal, really.

"Thanks so much for arranging that," I said. "Please ask him to call me so we can discuss his fee."

I was afraid his fee might break our budget. But I'd find a way to make it work somehow. It would be worth it.

"Oh, we already talked about that," Marcie said. "Gray said for us he'd be willing to perform for free. He said you can just consider it a donation in kind. It won't cost the choir anything, but he'd appreciate having the receipt for his taxes. Is that OK?"

OK? I thought. It's perfect! Out loud, I said:

"That's very generous, Marcie. Please thank him for me. And I'll be able to do that in person when he comes for the dress."

"That's the other thing," Marcie said. "Gray said he'll probably come to town a few weeks before the concert. So he'll be able to sit in on a few earlier rehearsals."

"That's really not necessary," I said. "We don't usually expect soloists to do that. Especially not ones of his professional calibre."

"Oh, don't worry about that," she said. "He's always liked Grayston. He's come to visit me here a few times since we started dating. He said he's looking forward to seeing it again, spending some time here."

I suspect it probably had more to do with wanting to spend more time with Marcie. But whatever. I'll take it.

"That's great, Marcie," I said. "I look forward to meeting him and getting to work with him. Please tell him that. And please thank him again for his kind offer. We really to appreciate it."

"I'm glad it's working out," Marcie said. "To be honest, I'm looking forward to having him around too. He's been on the road so much lately. And long-distance relationships suck."

"That they do."

"OK," she said. "I guess I'll see you in the morning for church. Bye!"

I ended the call and looked down at my shepherd/husky, who was lying quietly under my desk.

"Hey, Wolf!" I said. She raised her head and cocked an ear to one side. Her quizzical look.

"We got our hotshot soloist!" I said, excitement in my voice. "We've just elevated our *Messiah* production to a whole new level!"

Wolf cocked her head the other way and looked at me

expectantly. Since none of those words – 'hotshot,' 'soloist' or '*Messiah'* – was 'walk' or 'park' or 'cabin' or 'treat' or any of the dozen or so other words she knows (including occasionally 'Wolf! No!' and 'Drop it!'), she wasn't quite sure what to make of what I'd just said. But she caught the general tone enough to know I was happy about something. And that made her happy too. She thumped her tail on the floor and gave an excited little growl.

I felt like doing the same.

A small celebration was in order. And I knew a nice walk in the country would be just the thing.

"Hey, Wolf!" I said. She cocked her head at me again. "Cabin?"

That's one of the words she does know. And loves. Wolf jumped to her feet, tail wagging fully now, and added a chorus of happy husky yips and growls. Wolf doesn't really 'talk' the way some huskies do, but she can certainly make her opinion known. And in this case she was telling me I'd made the right choice. I put on the kettle to make a thermos of tea to take with me. Quickly I changed into some bush clothes, put on my sturdy walking boots, leashed up the dog and headed for the car in the Grandview's small underground parking garage. Back in its Jazz Age glory, the owner's Model T lived down there, but now only its ghost remains. Like other ghosts in my life.

Time to hit the road.

Chapter 7

Except the Lord build the house
their labor is but lost that build it.

– Ps. 127, v. 1

The weather wasn't the best for it, but what the heck. We had a few more hours before the early dark would start to set in.

For several years I've been building a little cabin – really nothing much more than a shack in the woods – on a small parcel of land my wife and I bought when we first got married. It was going to be our retreat from the city and from our respective hectic jobs. And until her tragic death that's what it was.

My wife, Jeri, and our little girl, Chelsea, were driving back into town from the cabin one night several years ago when a drunk driver in a big pickup weaved across the centre line and plowed into them, pushing Jeri's little car into a swamp beside the winding county road. They didn't survive. But then neither did the other driver, who smashed his truck into a rock cut. Old Testament justice, I guess.

The cabin and its land remain a refuge for me still, but driving there now on my own, even all these years later, I still get a stab of pain as I come upon what in my mind will always be "Jeri's curve." I love the cabin and the land. But her absence leaves a hole in my heart.

The cabin was a project we'd both relished taking on, building it by hand – with no electricity, we had to rely on tools powered by battery or our own elbow grease. Much of the material we scrounged or salvaged – partly because we had little money and partly in an effort to be more environmentally friendly.

The result, still very much in progress, is rustic, bordering on rudimentary: just one main room with a loft bed and a small bump-out for the kitchen. The shed roof is old barn steel. The walls are repurposed old barn board, which helps it blend in nicely with the surrounding trees. For basic needs, there's a biffy off in the woods. (Wolf, of course, gets to poop and pee anywhere she likes. Must be nice.)

After less than an hour on the road, Wolf and I arrived at I've always called "the land." One of its great virtues is its proximity to town – far enough away to be a welcome escape but still near enough to be readily attained. Wolf fairly leapt out of the car and began running around and rolling in the mixture of remaining snow, old leaves and mud. It's a messy time of year to be up here. Not as nice as the fall, but I'll take it. We set off on a walk.

In the lower northwest corner of the property in late spring – too early for this time of year – there's a small creek of runoff from winter snowmelt. By June it will have run out of song and speed, leaving behind only dead leaves stuck together by the heat.

But at its height our little brook feeds a beaver pond that, were it much bigger, one might charitably want to call a tiny lake. That's what the real estate listing had boastfully claimed: "Small lake on the property."

Yeah, right.

In spring and summer the mosquitoes and other bugs like the pond too. But it's far enough from the cabin that they're not too much of a bother, especially if there's enough of a breeze to keep them away. We coexist in a kind of guarded détente.

The beavers – those destructive developers of the natural world – had been busy all fall shoring up their dam of mud and sticks. Expanding, it seemed to me, the boundaries of their little domain and encroaching on a stand of birch trees on the east side of the pond. I thought of Frost's line about birches:

Earth's the right place for love:
I don't know where it's likely to go better.

He had that right.

I just hoped the beavers wouldn't drown those birches out of existence. But it's not like I could file a complaint with the township planning office. And besides, the beavers were here first. And at least so far as I knew they had no plans to erect a big condo tower to obstruct my view. I decided to leave them to their business.

Wolf always gets at least three times the exercise I do on our walks, running ahead and crossing the path back and forth as she explores to the sides, sometimes running back to me as if to say, "Hey, keep up with me! I've found all sorts of keen stuff!" After letting her gambol about for a while, I whistled for her so we could head back. She returned reluctantly, knowing what comes next. I put her on her leash. She wasn't happy about it, but it was already starting to get dark and there can be porcupines out foraging. You don't want to encounter one of them. Both shepherds and huskies have a high prey drive, and

I wasn't sure Wolf was disciplined enough to stay away from those painful quills.

Worse than that, last time I was up, the farmer down the road had warned me he'd seen a fisher in the area. Something like a weasel, only bigger and meaner, fishers – sometimes called fisher cats – are no pussycats but vicious mammals, with jaws that bite and claws that catch. A bit smaller than my dog, but I wouldn't bet against one in a fight. Just like people, looks can be deceiving. And the most dangerous ones aren't necessarily the most obviously so.

Grayston too knew something about deception. And weasels.

Safely back in the cabin, I fired up the woodstove and ate a sandwich I'd picked up before leaving town, with some tea from the thermos. Fine dining it wasn't. But even from a thermos, my own tea is better than anything I might have gotten at that drive-thru. Wolf ate some kibble, drank some water and then lay happily on the rug by the stove. She seemed to have forgiven me for the leash.

I read for a while, then took Wolf outside on her leash for a final pee before we had to head back home. Church in the morning, as always. We encountered no critters. But they were probably out there, beyond the glow of light coming from the cabin. One day maybe I'd install a solar panel, but for now I relied on batteries. Or candles in a pinch.

And the moon was just coming out, about three-quarters full, casting its own wash of light through the trees. What poets and pretentious writers – and no one else ever – call a gibbous moon. I suppose that makes me pretentious too for even knowing that term. But words are – or until recently were – my professional stock in trade. And knowing a lot of them

– even obscure, abstruse ones I'd never dare use in ordinary conversation – was part of the job. And sure, part of the fun.

Don't use a five-dollar word when a fifty-cent word will do, Twain advised. And by and large he was right. As Twain was right about most things. We all know writers who like to trot out their fancy vocabulary of big words – sesquipedalian circumlocutions, ha! – but mostly that just becomes annoying. The difference between playful enjoyment and just showing off, I guess. Is there a word for ostentatious that's less show-offy?

Much as I enjoy and even rely on the internet for quick access to information and keeping up with the news – it was getting hard to imagine how we managed without it before – it was also nice to take a break from all that technology and get back to simpler basics.

I had my cellphone with me in case of emergency, but I'd turned it off once I got to the woods. Fewer distractions. Even back in civilization I purposely avoid using my phone very much, if at all, to connect to the web. I have a desktop computer at home that serves me well enough. I like my smartphone for the convenience of calling and texting, taking pictures and listening to music. But I try not to be tethered to the web at all times the way some people are. Walking along, heads down, constantly staring at their phones, bumping into things. Like techno-zombies. Clueless to the world outside their little bubble.

Harlan Ellison once called television the "glass teat." Today you might as well apply that to smartphones.

As a veteran newsman – pardon me, newsperson – more than most I like to keep abreast of current events, both local and beyond, as I did especially when it was the core of my professional life. But still, it's good for the soul to take a breather once in a while, to slow down a pace. To get away, as transcendentalist writer Thoreau observed, from our lives of quiet desperation. (Though much as we might admire Thoreau and his idyllic life at Walden Pond, it's well to remember he was not nearly as self-sufficient as he claims. His shack in the woods was only about two miles from Concord, Mass. And far being solitary, Thoreau often walked into town to pick up supplies and hang out with friends. His mother, meanwhile, often provided him food and did his laundry. Another myth eroded, though not completely destroyed.)

I don't claim to be Thoreau. Nevertheless, I felt good about being even briefly out of the loop and out of the fray.

Chapter 8

High and low, rich and poor,
one with another.

– Ps. 49, v. 2

By Marcie's account, Grayston – the singer, not the city – was even more accommodating that I could have hoped. He'd cleared his schedule – his sked, as journalists would call it – to be available for the performance in May. But not only that, he'd also decided Grayston – the city, not the singer – would be a nice place to hang out leading up to the performance.

The countertenor, or male alto (alto being the generic term and as distinct from the contralto, or female alto), is a rare male voice that can have a wonderful, bright, clear sound when properly trained. It certainly would be historically accurate, given that the countertenor is often used in Baroque music. And Handel's debut performance of *Messiah* had not one but two male altos among its soloists. And only male altos (and boy trebles) in the choir.

Still, not everyone who calls himself a countertenor is truly up to the demands of the voice. Same for tenors and others, truth be told. But more so than any other voice, the male alto is at risk of losing vocal integrity at even the slightest sore throat or cold. (Basses are lucky – sometimes with a cold they just get to add a few notes on their bottom end.)

As a sometime countertenor myself, I know the hazards. One of the reasons that after graduating with my music degree I'd chosen a career path in what had seemed the more secure world of newspaper journalism (ha! little did I know) rather than as a fulltime choral musician or soloist.

I decided to share the good news – no, not *that* Good News – with Christine Tanaka, my fellow music director in Alliston.

"Hey, Chris," I said when she answered her phone and after some of the usual pleasantries. "I've found us an alto soloist."

"That's good, Dugan," she said. "Anybody I'd know?"

"Probably," I said. "It's Grayston Bergdorf."

She was silent for a moment.

"Grayston Bergdorf the countertenor," she said, somewhere between a statement and a question.

"Yes," I said. "That's him. That is he."

More silence. Was she processing our good luck? Or did she not like the idea of a countertenor? Not everyone does. Especially contraltos, who sometimes see them as competition. Their loss.

The silence stretched to a length that was getting uncomfortable. I was hoping I wouldn't have to fight her on this.

"Sorry, Dugan," she said after another moment. "I'm just a bit flabbergasted is all. That's terrific news! He's an incredible singer. I have some of his recordings."

"Glad you're happy," I said, relieved.

"Are you kidding?" she said. "He's an amazing get. How did you manage it? And can we afford him?"

So I told her the deal about Marcie and her boyfriend and Bergdorf agreeing to waive his usual fee. And that he'd even be around for a few rehearsals before the gig.

"Wow, that's great," Christine said. "What a relief. Now

we have all four soloists covered. I'll admit, my bass and soprano will have a hard time living up to the standard Bergdorf will set. But still, it will be great to have him on the program. Having a big name like that might even help us sell more tickets."

I'd thought of that too. We'd agreed to split proceeds from the concerts to put toward our respective music programs. These days of general cutbacks and declining congregations, it's getting harder and harder to fund our operations.

Not unlike newspapers losing readership and ad revenue. Why do I always seem to find myself in dwindling professions? 'Do what you love,' they always say, 'and the money will follow.'

Ya, right. What do *they* know?

Christine and I ended our call each, I think, newly excited by the prospect of this production we were mounting. And looking forward to sharing this news with our respective choirs at rehearsal before the service in the morning.

My choir took the news of our superstar soloist with excitement and relief. My contralto section lead, Meg, was especially relieved. She'd told me she'd been feeling guilty, that somehow she was letting us down because of her crazy workload. This made her feel better. Took the pressure off.

Christine, I found out later, had a harder time.

Chapter 9

The Lord said unto my lord,
'Sit thou on my right hand,
until I make thine enemies thy footstool.

– Ps. 110, v. 1

Our promising countertenor soloist showed up a few weeks later. Our rehearsals had been going well. Christine said hers were too. By now it was early March and the weather was starting to warm up. Pretty soon I'd be safe ditching the wetsuit for my early morning kayak outings.

It was a Thursday evening like so many others. A few snow flurries, but nothing to keep singers away from their appointed rounds. Some choir members were setting up the chairs as usual, others milling around, sitting or standing in small groups. Chatting, getting their music organized, sipping from their Dugan-approved water bottles (no clangy metal, no crinkly thin plastic, preferably nothing that would fall over and roll away). I was at the piano sorting through my own pile of music, looking at my rehearsal list to remind myself what needed the most work and what we could afford to leave til Sunday morning before the service.

Marcie Harding came up to me, holding hands with a young man in jeans, sneakers and a plaid shirt, with blond hair and a boy-next-door smile.

"Hey, Mr. Heywood," she said. "I brought someone for you to meet."

She smiled proudly.

"Dugan Heywood," she said, "this is Grayston Bergdorf. Gray, this is Mr. Heywood."

He reached out and we shook hands.

"Nice to meet you," I said. "Please call me Dugan."

"Likewise. Call me Gray."

From his looks and easygoing manner, you'd hardly know he was anything to write home about. He certainly didn't seem like the world-class concert soloist and recording artist I knew him to be. Still in his mid-20s, he'd already won several awards, worked with some of the top conductors and sung prestige roles in operas by Handel, Gluck and Britten. But from the look of him, he might have been just any recent university grad – or even someone just come to town from one of the farms in the countryside that surrounds Grayston. When I was the newspaper's Region editor, I'd met plenty of them while covering county fairs and council meetings.

"I thought I'd start sitting in on rehearsals, if that's OK with you," Gray said. "I can help out the section a bit and get a feel for how you want the music to go."

Hardly necessary, I thought to myself. Still, never look a gift countertenor in the mouth, I always say.

"Terrific," I said out loud. "We'd appreciate that."

I gestured over to my right. "The altos sit on that side, with the tenors behind. Sopranos and basses on the other side. I can introduce you, if you like."

"No need to fuss," he said. "I'll just find myself a seat. Marcie already set me up with the music for Sunday. Even my own cubbyhole to keep it in. My name on it and everything. And I have my copy of *Messiah* for later."

Smiling at Marcie, he went and grabbed an extra chair, placing it among my handful of altos. For her part, Marcie gave me a smile of her own before sitting down, as if to say, "See? I told you it would be great."

And she's right. It was.

Affable and easygoing, Gray Bergdorf seemed to slip easily into my alto section. If adding a countertenor was making any of the women altos feel threatened or resentful, no one was showing it. The younger women obviously found him cute and charming, if not downright dishy. The older ones seemed to be feeling more motherly about him. Or if not motherly, maybe more like a doting aunt.

Auntly? Seems unfair we don't have a word for that. Or maybe we do, but I sure don't know it. And I'm a word nerd. 'Avuncular' may not be a word that comes up often, but lots of ordinary people would know it means 'uncle-ish' or 'uncle-like.' There must be a similar Latin word for aunt and hence 'aunt-like' – but it doesn't seem to have made its way into common English usage. Too bad. And yet another example of how patriarchal and sexist English continues to be. I wonder if other languages have that 'aunt-less' problem too?

But I digress. As I am wont to do.

Gray was fitting in nicely not only socially but – more important – also musically. The countertenor voice is usually brighter (hell, sometimes even more strident) than the contralto. One of its charms for those of us who like it. One of its drawbacks, its critics would say. But Gray obviously had enough experience and tact to know how to blend in with the rest of the section. So I welcomed having him along. As we rehearsed the regular church stuff, he either already knew it or was a terrific sightreader. A little of both, I'd guess. It was clear he'd grown up singing church choir repertoire. And when it came time to rehearse *Messiah* – a work evidently he knew well – he brought a clarity of tone that added just the right amount of crispness to those long passages of runs. If he was willing to sing with the section in between his solo work, this was going to work out well. I'd have to make sure not to push him. Or I could just leave it up to him. After all, he knows his own voice best.

Sunday sorted, a few more pages of *Messiah* learned and/or rehearsed, we called it a night. Singers gathered up their music and dutifully stacked the chairs along the wall. Whether some church committee or one of several different kinds of community groups, someone was bound to be using the hall on Friday or Saturday before we returned for the service Sunday morning. I had a momentary twinge, remembering it was a late Friday night that our sexton, the church custodian Tom, had discovered Priya's body at the foot of the stairs over in the vestibule of the hall. I took a pause to banish the haunting memory.

Turning to Gray, I asked if he'd mind staying behind for a few moments to talk over, or even run though, some of his solo music.

"Sure," he said, but not before glancing at Marcie. She smiled back. A little proudly, it seemed to me, happy to stay and listen to her famous boyfriend before they walked back home to her place for a little alone time.

Chapter 10

Thou hast turned back the edge of his sword.

– Ps. 89, v. 42

After the orchestral overture (Handel calls it "*Sinfonia*"), the tenor soloist sets the mood of the narrative with the opening recitative, the conversational *Comfort ye my people*, followed by the solo aria *Ev'ry valley*. The choir has its first short chorus, *Glory to God*, followed by a declamatory bass recit, *Thus saith the Lord*. And then here's where it gets a bit tricky for the music historians – and especially the musical pedants. Of which there are more than a few.

For his first *Messiah* performance – not in London, as you might expect, but in Dublin, and not in a church but in a concert hall so crowded that the advertisements asked ladies not to wear hoop skirts and told gentlemen to leave their swords at home – Handel wrote a setting of the text "But who may abide the day of his coming?" But that was just another simple recit, sung again by the bass. The version we have now – the one everyone knows and sometimes gets into fights over – is a much more elaborate setting of *But who may abide* followed immediately by *For he is like a refiner's fire*. That section is fast, flashy and demanding of the soloist – and the players too.

This is the version our hotshot would be singing. If he could pull this off, he'd be more than worthy of our admiration. For my money, almost worth the price of admission alone. This is the version Handel wrote in London in 1750 for the Italian male alto Gaetano Guadagni. And it's become a standard benchmark for countertenors (and contraltos) ever since. A calling card. One of those solos by which you can make your mark.

But here's the controversy: Because of the bass recit that precedes it – and before the revival of the male alto voice in the 1950s (it had survived the 19th century in Anglican church choirs but not on the concert or opera stage) and then a greater emphasis on "historically accurate" performance starting in the '60s and '70s – *But who may abide/Refiner's fire* was often taken by a bass soloist. Alfred Deller and other countertenors brought the male alto voice back into vogue starting in the '50s. And now there's a healthy batch of topnotch countertenors giving concerts and making recordings. And wrenching *But who may abide/Refiner's fire* back from the hands of the basses. After all, as renowned *Messiah* editor Watkins Shaw says in the definitive 1958 Novello edition, Handel often reworked pieces as needed and had even transposed this one for a soprano. But "there is not one shred of evidence," Shaw says, "that he ever gave it to a bass." So there! That's OK – bass soloists get to show off again near the end of *Messiah* with *Behold I tell you a mystery* and *The trumpet shall sound*. They should be happy with that.

It was time to see what skills young Gray Bergdorf was bringing to the table.

"Thanks for staying," I said.

"No problem," Gray said. "Where shall we start?"

"Let's jump right in, shall we?" I said with a small grin. "Right into the fire, as it were."

"As it were," Gray said, with a grin of his own.

I sat down at the old Steinway workhorse and opened my score to No. 6 ("*Version I,*" as Shaw has it, *"the third to be composed"*), *But who may abide?*

Gray didn't even bother bringing his copy from the cubbyhole. He's sung it often enough to know it by heart.

It starts off simply enough – a slow, lilting D-minor waltz in 3/8. Simple enough that even I, with my rudimentary keyboard skills, could manage. (I'm slightly better at the computer keyboard than at the piano, if only because my long journalism career has afforded me more practice.) I knew it would get much harder – for me, at least – in another page or two.

Gray had done such a great job blending with the section – and I had the whole choir on my mind – that I hadn't really heard him properly during rehearsal. His voice definitely added a certain timbre to the section, but it was subtle. Now was my first chance to hear him on his own, other than recordings I'd already heard.

And man, it was impressive!

But who may abide the day of his coming
And who shall stand when he appeareth?

That opening leap of a downward fifth – the one I carry in my head and pull out whenever I need to remember what a downward fifth sounds like (an upward fourth is *Away in a Manger*) – and the phrase that followed was clear and sweet, with just a hint of sorrow and yearning, managing to convey so much emotion with so little effort.

After my treble voice changed, I sang many years as a countertenor, both in choirs and as a soloist – though lately, as I like to tease, I've been slumming and singing more tenor. And when I sang alto, if I may say so, I wasn't half-bad. But even on my best day, I couldn't hope to match the quality and musicality of what I was hearing from Grayston Bergdorf. It was all I could do to keep plunking away at the accompaniment. I could hardly wait for what was to come.

And Gray did not disappoint.

After "abiding" a bit more, we got to the next section, *For he is like a refiner's fire*. Handel marks it "*Prestissimo*" – which roughly translated is Italian for "you've got to be kidding me!" And with typical Handelian word painting, the music is fast and fiery, a chance for the soloist (and accompanying orchestra) to show off both leaps and agility. Gray sailed through it effortlessly, while I struggled to keep up.

We get a bit of a reprieve, and a reprise, with a return to the slow waltz, before Handel fires up the music again to finish off. It's traditional for the singer to close with a short, improvised cadenza – a little tag to show off with before the orchestra has the last word with the final eight bars. Gray was clearly having fun with his, an octave leap from F to high F, touching on a high G you'd have to give some of my choir sopranos danger pay to sing, before resolving on the D an octave higher than the one Handel has written in the score.

All in all, it was impressive – though never at any point anything less than tasteful and musical. I knew we'd found our perfect soloist for the part. I only hoped the other three – soprano, tenor and bass – would also each be bringing their A game.

"Well, that was amazing," I said, trying not to gush. "Are those tempos about where you want them to be? I'm sorry for my half-assed accompanying."

"Those tempos are fine," he said. "I like to have that stark contrast between the slow and fast sections. Really brings out the drama. And don't worry about your playing. It was fine."

He was being kind and we both knew it. But that's part of being a good musician – a good artist in any field – you have high standards, but you also play well with others. Better to be gracious than demanding. Nothing worse than a *prima donna* (or its male equivalent, the *primo uomo*, a term less a part of the vernacular). Gray knew he'd have good players in the orchestra when it came to the actual gig. For now, I was just there to make sure we were on the same page, as it were.

"I guess the only other big solo for me is *He was despisèd* near the start of Part II," Gray said. "We can go over that now, if you want. Or I'm happy to leave it til the dress. Whichever you prefer. Marcie tells me you're trimming it down with a bunch of cuts. I get that. Time is money. It's too bad, though. I'd love to also do *Thou art gone up on high*. It's a wonderful aria. And I so rarely get a chance to sing it."

"Ya, sorry about that," I said. "Not this time, I'm afraid. It is beautiful and I'd love to hear you sing it. But it's not one the orchestra usually has in its bag of tricks either. Maybe some other time."

"Just say the word and I'll come back for it," Gray said. "Anytime."

"I should let you and Marcie get home," I said. "I don't want to keep you. But I would love to ask you about your name – I mean beyond the coincidence of Grayston the singer and Grayston the town."

"You've probably figured it out already," he said. "My father named me after Grayston Burgess."

"The famous English countertenor. Well, one of them."

"Yes," he said. "And my dad was a countertenor too. A pretty good one."

"Father and son countertenors," I said. "Like Alfred Deller and his son Mark."

"Yes. My middle name is Alfred."

"I'm surprised he didn't name you Bowman – after James," I said.

"He wanted to," Grayston smiled. "My mother talked him out of it. She thought Bowman Bergdorf was a bit of a mouthful."

"Probably right."

And with that Marcie, who had been sitting quietly off to the side, came over and handed Gray his coat. It was time for them to go.

"Goodbye," I said. "Thanks again for staying behind. Have a good night. Marcie, I'll see you Sunday morning."

"You'll see us both," Gray said. They went out the door, leaving me to lock up.

Such a nice boy, I thought. No wonder my altos were doting on him.

Chapter 11

The same stone which the builders refused
is become the headstone in the corner.

– Ps. 118, v. 22

As a matter of historical fact, Grayston (the town) is named after some minor British functionary from pre-revolutionary times, back when the redcoats were still running things and haughtily naming towns, villages and various other landmarks after themselves. But for those of us who live here now, the running joke is that the town is named for all the grey stone – limestone and others whose names I don't know – that's abundant in the area. You'll find it in many of the town's municipal and other important buildings and many of its oldest homes, from simple worker's cottages and solid row townhouses to grand old mansions.

In the green, leafy shade of summer, and especially in the riotous colors of fall, all that grey stone sits in solid, elegant contrast. But in the cold of winter trying to become spring – where we were now – the grey stone and grey skies and the deep grey of the lake form a gloomy backdrop to which the bare trees add cold comfort.

The next few days were uneventful, as the best days often are. Mornings after a quick walk (and a sniff and a poop for Wolf) I shouldered my kayak and walked it around the corner and down to the lake for a quick paddle.

Most of the ice had melted but that left the water frigid, so a wetsuit was still in order. I may be gung-ho, but I'm not stupid. Not most of the time anyway. I love this early-morning time out on the water. The lake was calm, with nary a wave. Not enough wind to generate any beyond a gentle lapping along the shoreline. Later, by afternoon, the wind might have picked up enough to encourage a few hearty sailors or windsurfers to venture out from the yacht club even in water this cold.

Better them than me, says I. I'm happy in the relative safety of my 13-foot fibreglass kayak and its double-bladed paddle. Sitting low, the kayak stays stable even in the roughest water. And if worse comes to worst, if a big swell knocks me over, I can usually roll myself back up. As I've had to do a few times – a lot more fun in the summer's heat than the winter's chill. So, wetsuit and life jacket it was. Better safe than sorry.

I was heading west, away from downtown and toward the college campus and hospital, keeping my course close to shore in the relatively shallow water. My kayak blade is the older kind, with its flat blades set at a 90-degree angle. The newfangled ones the kids have are often a bit curved and both face the same direction. Makes no sense to me, but I guess it's whatever you're used to. After all, how many hundreds (thousands?) of different strains of Christianity are there? And who's to say who's right? Is anyone?

Anyway, with my offset paddle, after you've finished your stroke on one side, you have to do a little flick of the wrist so your blade on the other side meets the water flat on and not on its thin edge. If you miss – at best your stroke has no power, at worst you risk losing your balance. But just like music, with practice you get used to it and it becomes automatic, a muscle memory you no longer have to put much brain power into. Which I like because it leaves my brain free to think about other things.

Sometimes those thoughts might even be profound. Other times, not so much. But for me it's almost a form of meditation. Maybe that's why other people pray.

Dip. Pull. Wrist.

Dip. Pull. Wrist.

My own form of litany.

Without thinking about it, I found my paddling had fallen into something close to the easygoing rhythm of the opening phrase of Grayston Bergdorf's solo aria from the night before. A lilting 3/8 but basically one beat to the bar:

But who may abide the day of his coming
And who shall stand when he appeareth?

I began to sing it through in my head. (Not out loud. No point waking the neighbors. It was still early morning, the sun barely up from the horizon.) I remembered Gray's effortless delivery and full-bodied yet sweet tone. Clearly this was a young countertenor with a bright future ahead of him. We were lucky to have scored him when we did. It made me even more hopeful for the success of our little musical project. I just hoped the other singers in the choir – the other soloists but especially our combined alto forces – saw having a singer of his calibre join us not as competition, but as opportunity. A chance to improve themselves by learning from the best.

By now in my head I'd gotten to the flashy *prestissimo* section of the aria, which moves into 4/4 from the previous 3/8.

For he is like a refiner's fire
And who shall stand when he appeareth?

But interestingly, without having to speed up, the underlying pulse – what fancy musicians call the *tactus* – remains the same one in a bar. Even in the Baroque, Handel was using an old Renaissance trick of alternating between triple and duple meters while keeping the same beat, the same *tactus*. I'd have to tell the choir that at our next rehearsal. Maybe they'd find it interesting.

Or maybe I'm just a music geek as well as a word nerd.

By now I'd paddled past the campus. A few brave students were running along the shore path by the two big waterfront sculptures, *Blobby* and *Spikey*. (I know they have proper artsy names, but that's what everyone calls them.) It was time to turn back and get on with my day. Not that I had much planned. I looked forward to a glorious, easy day of futzing and puttering around. Take Wolf for a longer walk before the rain they were forecasting. Sometimes they even got that right.

With a deft couple of strokes – one forward, one back – I swung *Assignment* around and headed back home. (I named my kayak *Assignment*. An old newspaper joke: "Sorry, Dugan's not here. He's out on *Assignment*.")

Dip. Pull. Wrist.

Dip. Pull. Wrist.

This is the kind of serenity I could easily abide.

Chapter 12

Mine enemies go about all the day long to swallow me up,
for they be many that fight proudly against me.

– Ps. 56, v. 2

The rest of Friday and Saturday flew by apace and once again it was Sunday morning. I gave Wolf a quick walk and changed from my scruffy dogwalking duds into something a little more respectable for the congregation. No point giving the naysayers any more ammo than they already think they have.

The service went easily – Lenten services are sparse by design. I was pleased to see Gray Bergdorf chatting amiably (but quietly) with those around him as we lined up at the back of the church to process in. We'd finally managed to finish the glassed-in atrium to connect the church hall with the church proper (and thereby hangs a tale), so we managed to keep dry from the cold rain that had finally come overnight. The weather forecasters were right, if off by only a day and a half. Someone – probably Marcie – had fitted Gray with a spare blue cassock and white surplice (a surplus surplice), so he fit right in with the rest of the choir.

I confess I barely heard a word of Hugh Parry's sermon – I was too busy setting and reminding myself of organ stops for the postlude that ends the service – so I hope he wasn't going to quiz me on it afterward. I often duck out without staying for the post-service coffee hour – I have better tea at home – but Hugh had asked me to stay behind so we could discuss something.

That sounded ominous.

In fact the news was better than I'd feared – a reminder to myself not to worry so much.

"Besides thanking you, as always, for the music," the minister said, "I just wanted to let you know that I've been making some headway with some of the – shall we say – less enthusiastic members of the musical search committee."

"Thanks," I said, sipping my tea, by now lukewarm. "I appreciate your support."

"Well, you know how some of those old Episcopalians can be," Hugh said. "Fancy themselves all high church – at St. Quentin's, mind you, a tiny parish church in a small city not much bigger than a small town! Lord, help us!"

"Yes," I said with a smile I hoped was not too snarky, "some of them have delusions of adequacy."

Hugh snorted out some of his coffee, which nearly brought on a coughing fit and drew too much attention to us hiding off in the corner away from the rest of the small crowd.

Recovering as much priestly aplomb as he could manage, Hugh gave me a small, forgiving smile.

"What can I say, Dugan?" he said. "Some of them seem to think that if you aren't wearing a hairshirt and thrashing your back, you're not penitent enough for their liking. And they generally know you're not, shall we say, a full member of the tribe. God knows I know from our many discussions that you're in fact better versed in theology – and frankly, if I may say, a better Christian – than many of the so-called Christians among my congregation. But try explaining to them the nuanced difference between an agnostic and an atheist."

"*Mea culpa*," I said. "Wolf generates a lot of hair. Maybe I could weave it into something wearable?"

That almost brought on another snort.

"Don't worry," Hugh said. "I've managed to bring most of them onside. In fact I think I've winnowed it down to one final holdout. I've stressed the important fact that I'm the one in charge of the liturgy, while you're in charge of the music. The two don't always have to be in perfect, um, harmony. And that you've always gone along with any musical or liturgical requests I've made of you.

"And besides," he said, "I told them that, with poor old Bill Garner unable to perform his duties, we were lucky to have found you – a musician of your obvious skill – on such short notice."

"My blushes, Watson!"

"Even more than that," Hugh grinned conspiratorially, "when in doubt, appeal to their wallets. I reminded them that, by comparison to anyone else we might be able to hire with your level of experience and ability, we were paying you a mere pittance."

"I've been meaning to mention that," I said. But I smiled, I hoped, disarmingly.

"Don't worry," Hugh said, smiling back. "Once I've roped them all in, I hope to get you a small raise too."

"Thanks. I mean that. I'd never turn down a raise. But I'll understand if it doesn't happen. I know things are tight."

"Just leave that to me," Hugh said. "And meanwhile, I'll keep working on old Mrs. Grundy."

With a final smile, Hugh turned and left. Off to schmooze some actual congregant.

I wonder if Mrs. Grundy really is the name of the holdout?

I was about to leave too when I saw a somewhat imposing woman in, I would say, her 50s, all made up and decked out in a fancy dress and a gaudy necklace. She was headed right for me, like an ocean liner about to swamp my little kayak. I braced for impact.

"Are you Dugan Heywood?" Her tone, while not completely confrontational – yet – was more than one of mere polite coffee hour inquiry. This woman had something on her mind.

"Yes," I said, conjuring another disarming smile. "I am. How may I help you?"

"I wish to speak to you about my daughter."

As a younger man – especially as a teenager – that kind of phrase might strike fear in one's heart. But since I've long been widowed and haven't even dated anyone for a few years, I felt I was reasonably safe. As for my women and girl choristers, my behavior with them has been entirely beyond reproach. I'm sure of it.

"I'm sorry," I said, "I don't know your name. Have we met before?"

"No, we have not," she said, dialing the umbrage back only one notch. "My name is Mrs. McBride, Margaret McBride. My daughter, Cassandra, sings at St. Andrew's Presbyterian Church in Alliston."

"Oh," I said, "she sings in Christine Tanaka's choir?"

"Yes," she said, "with *Ms.* Tanaka."

I thought I detected a note of disdain on the "Ms." Great – she was one of those. I only hoped she wasn't also disdainful of the "Tanaka" not being WASPy enough for her liking.

I have no time for racism. Or sexism. Or most other kinds of "-isms."

If there's a God, God protect me from zealots.

Mrs. McBride, dressed in her Sunday best rather more formally than I'm used to seeing in our modest parish church, gave me a look of cool disdain. Obviously my chinos and open-neck shirt (I don't like wearing ties) barely met with her approval. At least I was wearing a blazer.

"Yes," I said, "I remember Cassandra from our first combined rehearsal last month. Lovely voice."

"Well, thank you I'm sure," Mrs. McBride said, her tone softening a bit at the compliment. Maybe I'd win her over yet.

"She pays attention. And a good sightreader," I said. "An alto with promise, I think."

"A *contr*alto," Margaret McBride said, bringing more gravitas and imperious dignity to the term than I might have imagined could apply to a young woman who was maybe only 16 years old, if that.

"What I want to know from you, Mr. Heywood," she said, "is since – as even you admit – my daughter has such a 'lovely' voice, why you didn't choose *her* to be your *Messiah* soloist, instead of that dreadful *countertenor*!"

Dreadful countertenor? Best let that slide for the moment.

"We *did* consider your daughter, Mrs. McBride," I said, as politely as I could manage. "Both Christine and I. We gave her a full audition. In which she performed quite well, I will say."

Mrs. McBride gave a brief smile. But whether to acknowledge the genuine compliment or merely to confirm her own bias it was hard to say.

"Then why not choose her?" she said. "Why bring in this *outsider*?"

Did I really want to explain all this? Did I really have to? That Cassandra's voice – though indeed, yes, lovely – is still too small, and she's still too unsure of herself, to take on such a big and demanding solos? As Christine had said to me privately, Cassandra could barely even manage a small solo in the context of a church anthem. She'd need more experience to overcome her nerves and natural shyness.

At her audition, we'd thanked Cassie for her efforts, praised her musicianship and told her, as gently as we could, that we thought she just wasn't ready for a leap to the big time. (If you can even call one performance each in Grayston and Alliston the big time.)

Cassie, it had seemed to both Christine and me at the time, was if anything relieved. As if trying out for the big alto solos had been not her own idea, but her mother's. Being confronted now by Margaret McBride, I decided that was probably true. I've heard of pushy stage mothers, but I'd never encountered one before in the world of church music. I guess I shouldn't be surprised.

Mrs. McBride was talking again. She'd softened her tone – a little more pleading than demanding.

"– and I really think you should give her another chance," she was saying. "She was fighting a bit of a cold that day of the audition. She wasn't really at her top form. My husband agrees with me. You were terribly unfair to her."

"I'm sorry, Mrs. McBride," I said, "Christine and I both agree Cassandra's not quite ready for such a big role. Her voice is fine and she's clearly a good musician. Christine says she's wonderful in the choir. But her voice is still maturing. It isn't big enough, and she's not yet confident enough, for the *Messiah* solos. Even she seemed to think so."

"Oh, Cassandra doesn't know what's best for her career," her mother sniffed dismissively. "But *I* do. And so does her father. You just don't see it."

"I'm sorry –" I was doing a lot of apologizing. But Mrs. McBride wouldn't even let me finish.

"You can take your apology and stuff it somewhere," she said. angry again. "I just think it's terrible that you'd give solos to a man – to an *abomination* who sings in such a silly high voice – instead of to a beautiful, promising young woman, for whom Mr. Handel obviously wrote his music in the first place."

Abomination? Should I let her get away with that insult? To Grayston Bergdorf in particular and to my fellow countertenors in general? As for Handel composing sacred music for women singers, did I really want to get into a whole TED talk with this foolish woman about Handel – or indeed most "classical" composers before about the mid-18th century – and the centuries-long history of male voices in sacred music and the relatively late entry of women?

That long history may be patriarchal and unfair, but it's also undeniably factual – whether we like it or not.

Discretion being the better part of running away and hoping to fight another day, I bit my tongue. Decided against getting into a pointless squabble.

"I'm sorry, Mrs. McBride," I said again in my most sincere tone. ("Sincerity is everything!" Sam Goldwyn used to say. "If you can fake that, you can fake anything!")

"I hope we'll do *Messiah* again next year too," I said. "Maybe by then Cassie will be more than ready."

"*Next* year?" Mrs. McBride huffed. "I'm not even sure Cassandra wants to sing it *this* year after being so insulted!"

With that and without another word, she turned about and steamed off, her imposing presence parting the remaining parishioners as she approached and leaving them slightly cowed in her wake.

Chapter 13

They lie waiting in our way on every side,
watching to cast us down to the ground.

– Ps. 17, v. 11

I gave Wolf a longer walk when I got home and checked her food and water, but decided against an afternoon paddle. Maybe I'd try for early evening.

Home for the past several years since my wife and daughter died has been a condo apartment in the Grandview, a grand old Victorian lady of stately red brick that started as a private mansion, then became a popular hotel in the Jazz Age before rising and falling in respectability over the next several decades. I'd lived there as a student and briefly after graduating, when it was a cheap and cheerful bohemian enclave of students, struggling artists, other artsy types and a few charming oddballs. (I might have been one of those.) In those distant days I had a one-room bedsit with a bathroom but no kitchen – just a hotplate and bar fridge. I washed my dishes in a small plastic tub with water from the bathtub. It wasn't much, but I loved it.

Feeling flush with an actual salary, I moved to a "nicer" (and more expensive) apartment after landing my first fulltime job at the *Gazette*, which had launched my memorable but rudely curtailed newspaper career. In hindsight, I should have stayed longer at the old Grandview and saved up my nickels. But I've always been better at words than numbers.

Figuring she'd be home from her church gig about the same time as me, I called Christine.

"Hey, Christine, it's Dugan," I said after she'd picked up.

(Do you really 'pick up' a cellphone? Anyway, whatever.)

"You'll never guess who I bumped into after church today," I said. "Or rather, who nearly plowed into me."

"Let me guess," she said. I swear I could hear a smirk in her voice. "Margaret McBride."

"Right first time."

"Yes, she told me she wanted to 'have a word' with you. About Cassie, obviously, and why we didn't choose her as our alto soloist."

"That's the gist of it."

"I'm so sorry, Dugan," Christine said. "I should have warned you. She's a bit of, um, an imposition."

"That's one way of putting it."

"It's Cassie I worry about," she said. "She's really a sweet girl. Or at least that's how she comes across to me. I think even she knows she's not ready for this."

"So this is just a case of having a pushy mother?"

"Well, that for sure," Christine said. "But in her heart I think Margaret means well. She's just a bit, let's say, determined.

"In what ways?"

"As much as tiny Alliston can manage – you know how it is – Mrs. McBride fancies herself as a mover and shaker in town," Christine said. "A beacon of culture in our little backwater. Sits on the library board. Runs what passes for our arts council. Little musical talent herself, to be frank, but sees great things in store for her daughter.

"Maybe that's not so bad," I said.

"Just between you and me, Christine said, "it's Cassie's father who scares me more."

"What about him bothers you?"

"Mr. McBride – Harold – comes from rougher stock, you might say."

"Not very artistic?"

"At the risk of indulging in lazy stereotypes, not really," Christine said. "He runs a little repair shop out of their small farm on the edge of town. You know – fixes chainsaws, lawnmowers, that sort of thing. A bit of a mechanic on the side too. Always fixing something. Mrs. McBride's a bookkeeper for a few small businesses in town. And I presume also does the books for the family farm and repair business."

Bookkeeper, I thought in one of my magpie mind's unbidden trivia tangents. The only English word with three sets of double letters in a row. More useless information.

Forcing my brain back on track, I said: "So how does that bother you?"

"I don't know," Christine said. "They're just an odd pair. She aiming for high society and he rarely able to get the grease out from under his fingernails."

"I see," I said, not quite seeing but feeling I had to say something.

"Don't get me wrong," she said. "I barely know him. He rarely comes to church, even to hear his daughter sing. But the few times he *has* come, you can tell he's proud of her, even if he doesn't do a very good job of showing it. And fiercely protective. In some ways even more so than her mother."

"Really? How so?"

"Maybe it's just his manner. But he's a bit gruff with Cassie. With his wife too. I think there's a hot temper lurking not far under the surface. I would *not* want to be a teenage boy hoping to ask Cassie out on a date. At least I'd want to make sure I got her home safe and on time. I might fear for my life otherwise."

"You think he could be abusive? Maybe a mean drunk?"

"Maybe," Christine said, "though I've never seen any overt evidence of it.

"I heard a story from my daughter," she said. "They're about the same age and my daughter knows her from school and of course choir. They're not close friends, but you know how it is in a small town – you don't have a lot of options for other kids to hang out with.

"Anyway," she said, "some boy finally got up his courage to ask Cassie to a school dance. I think she was still 15. He must have been just 16 at the time, with a fresh new driver's licence. The boy – I know him, he's a sweet kid – gets all dressed up, borrows his dad's car and arrives at the McBride farm to pick up Cassie. Who of course is still getting ready."

I could imagine a teenage girl fretting over what must have been one of her first real dates.

"So the boy's standing there awkwardly," Christine says, "with, you know, gruff-looking Harold McBride giving him the once-over."

Been there, I thought. Done that. A scary prospect for a teen boy.

"So Cassie's dad says to him. 'While we're waiting, come out to the barn and give me a hand with something.'"

"Wow," I said. "The kid must have been panicking. Like something from a horror movie."

"Yes," Christine said. I could hear a bit of a smile in her voice. She was having fun telling this story. "So they go out to the barn. McBride has a cow and some goats and a few pigs. Some hens and chickens. Just enough to help feed his family, sell a few eggs sometimes.

"He picks up one of the young pigs – a young male – and says to the boy, 'Here. You hold him down while I get my cleaver.' So the kid – who's a townie, not a farm boy – is trying to hold onto this pig while it's squirming around. Both he and the pig scared witless.

"McBride says, 'Put him on that old stump and hold him still. I'm going to castrate him.' And as he's raising up a big knife, he says, 'Oh – and by the way – you'll have my daughter home by 11. Right?'"

"Jeez!" I said. "The poor kid must have crapped his pants."

"Not actually, but pretty much," Christine said. "Anyway, he dropped the pig. Nearly fainted himself. McBride managed to catch it and put it back in its pen, still intact. And then they went back to the house."

"So maybe he just wanted to scare the kid," I said. "Would have scared me at that age. Even now."

"Yes," Christine said. "I think it was more performative than serious. But word got around the school pretty quickly that Cassie McBride – and especially her father – is not someone you'd want to cross in any way."

If she were still alive, my own daughter would be not far off from that age where she'd be starting to think about dating boys. Or maybe girls. Either way, I know how guarded of her I'd be feeling as she started to venture out into the big, scary world on her own. I might not approve of McBride's shock tactics, but I have some understanding of how protective a father – or any parent – would be of their child.

"Did the boy ever ask her out on another date?"

Christine chuckled. "I don't think so. And I'm pretty sure he got her home safely well before 11."

"Poor Cassie," I said. "It must be tough having such a controlling father."

"Yes, I imagine so," Christine said. "But I will say, in his defence, that despite the rough edges he can be decent. And he does have a talent for repairing things."

"Really?"

"Oh sure," she said. "Picking Cassie up from choir one night he noticed my car had a scrape on one of the fenders. Little mishap in the grocery store parking lot. Frankly, I was just going to leave it. But he offered to fix it up and repaint it for me. Did a perfect job. You'd never know."

"Well, points for him."

"I mean it," she said. "With our music and our literature and our book learning, we may consider ourselves artists and cultured and all that. And of course we are. But on his own turf, with a grinder and spray paint, Harold McBride is as much a sculptor, as artistic a craftsman, as any of us."

"A good reminder to be humble," I said.

"Indeed."

Back on track, Christine and I cleared up a few more details about our plans for the coming week. We'd decided her choir would come to Grayston to join our rehearsal on Thursday, another chance for the two choirs to get used to singing together. For the first half, my choir would run through our Sunday music as usual in Macmillan Hall while the Alliston choir rehearsed its own stuff in the sanctuary. Which would also let them get a feel for the space where we'd be performing one of our two joint concerts. After the break, we'd both be in the sanctuary to rehearse *Messiah* and also to figure out who would go where. Sitting and standing arrangements are sometimes almost as much of a challenge as the music itself.

The following week, the St. Quentin's gang would troop to Allison and do the same routine in Christine's church. Rather than the hassle of carpooling, each of us had arranged to rent a schoolbus for the singers and for any parents or spouses who wanted to come along for the ride.

Assuming Cassie didn't drop out, I was sure Margaret McBride would be a watchful eye among them.

Chapter 14

Behold, how good and joyful a thing it is
for brethren to dwell together in unity!

– Ps. 133, v. 1

Thursday came around quickly, as Thursdays for choir directors tend to do. In what had become something of a pleasant routine, I'd had an early breakfast Monday morning with Sandra Novak, a former *Gazette* colleague and one of my few remaining regular contacts at the old newsroom. Lucky for her, Sandra had so far managed to avoid the 'restructuring' chopping block. Or maybe unlucky, since as one of the few staffers left standing she was usually run off her feet.

We met as usual and of course at Maggie's, the old diner that for more decades than I've been alive has occupied the building next door to the paper and across from the back of city hall. Which makes it a frequent meeting spot for newspaper hacks, city politicians, local movers and shakers and the student population alike – though those various and sundry groups don't much overlap.

Maggie's is something of an institution in Grayston. And also known as The Best Greasy Spoon in the Known Universe* (*Trademark pending.) Sandra and I had a more or less standing date for Monday morning breakfast, a chance for me to catch up on the latest inside scoop or for each of us to lament the generally sorry state of the world. And of our profession (my old profession) in particular.

I'd spent the rest of the time in between with the usual mix – walking the dog, some kayaking, practising (both music for Sunday and brushing up on some *Messiah* bits), even the routine of doing the laundry and cleaning the apartment. Amazing how you can fill your days even when you're not working full time. How the hell had I managed to do any of this when I was spending eight hours – sometimes more – every day at the job?

I have to say, I do like the more relaxed pace. I miss the money though. Sometimes the people. But not the grind.

The nice thing about a job at the newspaper was, well, the news. Every day brought something new and even the hope of something interesting: A little chicanery at city hall. Some other politician saying something stupid or outrageous. A coup in Chad. Those kept things fresh. I miss that.

But of course, like any job, there was also routine, boring stuff: Editing the horoscopes and syndicated advice column and the obits. Covering council meetings, compiling the weekly calendar of upcoming events, Gripping stuff, that. I don't miss that part of the daily slog.

Well, I suppose you can say the same of any job, including that of the church musician. "Oh, it's the feast of St. Whoosis again? I guess we'll have to trot out that hymn nobody likes very much."

At least as a journalist I've had my fair share of interesting, even exciting (and sometimes horrible) moments amid the long stretches of daily routine. More so than most jobs, I think. As John le Carré puts it in *The Honourable Schoolboy*: "Airline pilots, journalists, spies … It's the same drag. Bloody inertia interspersed with bouts of bloody frenzy."

Anyway, Thursday came and Christine's choir arrived from Alliston in its rented schoolbus. All sorts of groups from cub scouts to quilting bees make use of our church hall and/or sanctuary many times through the week. I can never keep track of who's where when.

And this day was no exception. As singers from the two choirs were entering, there was another group of adults in Macmillan Hall just wrapping up whatever kind of meeting they were having. I have no idea what it was, but the result was a much larger number of people milling around and either coming in or going out the door.

The Alliston choir, though a little smaller, has much the same makeup as mine – a mixed group of adults and teens, even a few kids of eight to 12 with promising voices. They may not contribute much to the overall sound, but it's good to start them early, get them enthusiastic before they become too distracted by the lure of team sports or video games.

Christine's husband had come along for the ride – a chance to spend more time with her and help out where he could. I was glad to see him, having met him only once before, when Christine and I first began to hatch this crazy collaboration scheme over her kitchen table in Alliston.

Also alighting from the bus – and looking none too happy for having endured it – was the indomitable Margaret McBride, her daughter Cassandra meekly in tow. I hoped I wouldn't have to confront Mrs. McBride again, especially in front of all the other singers.

Across the room, I gave Christine a quizzical look. She gave me back a wan smile and a small shrug, as much as to say, "Sorry. Not much I could do about it."

Whatever. Time to get this show on the road.

"Hello, everyone," I said to the singers milling around.

They quieted down, most of them ready to listen. Sometimes that's the best you can hope for.

"St. Andrew's singers, welcome to St. Quentin's. I'm Dugan Heywood, the music director here. I hope your bus ride was easy. At least most of the snow is gone.

"I want to thank Christine Tanaka for helping me organize this joint concert. I know my choir is really looking forward to singing with you."

"Us too!" Christine said with a smile, sparking some friendly sounds from the room.

"I'm sure you know the drill," I said. "For the first hour we'll rehearse separately for our own church music. My choir will be here in the hall as usual. You guys will be next door in the church.

"We have a lovely new glassed-in walkway that will take you there," I said gesturing to the door across the room to my right, "so you can stay nice and warm and dry. There's a cloakroom over there" I pointed to the other side "for your coats and boots. And washrooms if you need them before we start."

Some choristers began moving over to the cloakroom – little more than a long pole set in the wall with hangers for their coats, a shelf above for hats, scarves and gloves. Before I lost them completely, I continued:

"We'll have a break in the middle for some coffee, tea and juice," I said. "And even some cookies." This brought some smiles from the younger kids, as I knew it would.

"After that, we'll join you in the sanctuary to spend the rest of the night on *Messiah*. If you forgot yours and anyone needs a copy, we have a few extras over where my singers have their cubbyholes. You should find some in the bottom right-hand corner."

After a few more moments of people milling around the area of coats and cubbyholes, the confusion subsided and the Alliston singers trooped off to the church to rehearse.

Chapter 15

O praise the Lord, for it is a good thing to sing praises unto our God: yea, a joyful and pleasant thing it is to be thankful.

– Ps. 147, v. 1

At the break, one of my longtime tenors, Bill, as he has for years, helpfully provided tea, coffee, juice and cookies, which he conjures up from the church hall kitchen. Singers put spare change in a jar to help defray costs. In this case, I contributed a few extra bucks to cover for the guest choir. Singers from both choirs mingled around, introducing themselves, in some cases reconnecting with old friends and generally having a friendly visit.

Christine and I were off to one side huddled over our scores, deciding which movements, and which particular tricky bits, we were going to rehearse. We'd finalized most of this already by emails, so this was just touching base briefly. At Christine's request, we'd also decided I'd do the bulk of the conducting, since Christine didn't feel as confident at conducting an orchestra. But we'd agreed she could have the fun of conducting the crowd-pleasing *Hallelujah* chorus. I was happy to let her have that old chestnut.

From our spot at the piano, I could see Cassie over by the cubbyholes against the back wall chatting with Gray Bergdorf. Obviously she'd managed to overcome her natural shyness enough to speak with him. It didn't take long to see why: From her smiles and general awkwardness, it seemed pretty clear to me that, while Gray was being politely friendly, Cassie was smitten by his charm – even if he wasn't aware of that. I nudged Christine to take a look. She gave a small smile and nod. As a mother of a teenage girl about Cassie's age, she could see it too.

Just as I was wondering where the indomitable Mother McBride might be, she hove into view, having come back from the direction of the vestibule and atrium that leads to the church.

She stood for a moment scanning the room, then stopped when she saw Cassie and Gray speaking together. She didn't look happy with what she saw.

Making a beeline for her daughter, she took Cassie somewhat roughly by the hand. But not before shooting a withering look at Gray.

"Come along, Cassandra," she said, loudly enough that I could hear it across the room and above the general murmur. "Stop all this talking. You'll strain your voice. And besides, you should be looking over your music."

Almost dragging her, she led Cassie away and back toward the church.

It was time for us to end the break anyway and get back to work.

"Hello, choir!" I said, trying to get their attention. Someone – one of their basses, I think – gave a shrill whistle, the kind where you put your fingers in your mouth and blow. The room became suddenly quiet. I was grateful. I can't whistle like that and was about to break out the literal dogwhistle I carry on my keychain in case Wolf has galloped off too far in the park.

"Thanks," I said. "Let's move over to the sanctuary and get ourselves set up."

"I have a rough seating plan," Christine said to the room. "So come with me and I'll get you organized."

Grayston Bergdorf was standing at the cubbyholes looking a little confused. I went over to see him.

"I can't find my music," he said, rooting through the cubbyhole with his name on it. "I have all my Sunday stuff, but my copy of *Messiah* seems to have gone missing."

"Maybe you took it home?"

"No," he said, "I left it here last Thursday."

"Was it one of ours," I said, "or your own copy?"

"My own copy. I've used it for years. Has a bunch of my markings."

"Sorry about that. When did you see it last?"

"Let me think," Gray said. "I guess it's been more than a year. I didn't actually have a *Messiah* gig this past Christmas, but I did the year before. So until last week I guess it's been about a year and a half. It's just been sitting in my apartment at home. Most choirs don't do it in spring, you know."

"Don't I know it," I said. "What the hell was I thinking doing it so soon after Easter?"

"You were hoping to avoid the Christmas rush," he said, "when everyone else does it."

"Yes, that was part of it," I said. "Plus I thought it would be interesting to have our performance coincide more closely with the first time Handel did it, in April 1742. Silly me."

"Not silly at all," Gray said. "I think it's cool."

"Thanks. Anyway, I see there are still a few extra copies down there. Just grab one of those – though I warn you, you might be stuck with one of those old 1902 Ebenezer Prout editions, not the newer, more scholarly Watkins Shaw."

"Oh, quirky old Prout!" Gray said. "That might be fun. Did you know he wrote silly little lyrics to help him remember all 48 fugues of Bach's *Well-Tempered Clavier*?

I haven't seen Prout's *Messiah* edition in years. Not that it really matters. Pretty much have the whole thing memorized anyway. But I wanted my own copy to add any markings that you may want. Never mind, I'll make do for now."

"Great. Meantime, I'll keep an eye out for yours."

When Gray and I got to the sanctuary, Christine had the choir pretty much organized and standing in sections on the chancel steps in front of the altar and the side pews where the choir normally sits for the service. Choir stalls, they're called – which I always find amusing since it reminds me of horses. (Horses, as the old joke goes, are sometimes easier to train.) Gray politely squeezed himself in among the back row of altos. Cassie was in the front row, front and centre of the section. I wondered if Christine had put her there as a sop to her meddling mother. Mrs. McBride sat alone at the back, from what I could see alternately beaming at her daughter, glowering at Gray and scowling down at something in her lap. Maybe checking messages or texting someone on her phone.

Did Cassie look disappointed that she didn't get to stand anywhere near Gray? Maybe I just imagined it.

Chapter 16

The kings of the earth rise up
and the rulers take counsel together.

– Ps. 2, v. 2

Christine and I had decided for this rehearsal we'd cover as much as we could of *Part I*, since it has several choruses that feature the choir – including the cussedly fast and tricky one that closes the first part, *His yoke is easy*. Or as many choristers call it, *His yoke is anything BUT easy*.

And since for the first time we had all four soloists in the room, I thought it would be nice to give them a moment to strut their stuff, while for now remaining at their places within the choir, not out front as they would be for the actual performance. Less disruptive that way. There wasn't enough time to let them sing their full movements, but I knew the choir would enjoy hearing at least what we call "tops and tails" – the start and finish of each bit. Especially the final bars, since those often lead directly into the next chorus and the choir needs to be ready to stand up and sing.

And so our St. Quentin's tenor, Jordan Baxter, started off with the opening bars of his recit *Comfort ye*, the beautiful placid statement that comes after the orchestral opening. That earned him a smattering of polite applause and stamping of feet (which musicians sometimes do if they have music or an instrument in their hands and so cannot clap). He then went right to the closing bars of *Ev'ry valley*, which led the choir right into its first chorus, *And the glory of the Lord.*

Next came Gerry Roxton, the St. Andrew's bass, with a snippet of his declamatory recit *Thus said the Lord*, thus setting up Grayston Bergdorf's *But who may abide?* After a few bars, Gray skipped ahead to the end of his impressive, showy cadenza of *Refiner's fire,* which leads to the chorus *And he shall purify,* a nice bit of linkage in the text by Charles Jennens (in that quirky British way, pronounced 'Jennings'), who stitched together a wide assortment of *Bible* verses for Handel to tell the story. From where I was standing facing the choir, I could see Gray's girlfriend Marcie beaming with pride and Cassie's reaction too – which to my eye seemed a mix of awe and jealousy. With my back to Cassie's mother, there was no way for me to gauge her reaction. Maybe she was avoiding him by occupying herself on her phone, or whatever it was in her lap.

After that and a few cuts came the chorus *For unto us a child is born.* You can tell Handel was not yet entirely comfortable in English, his second language, since the music awkwardly puts the stress on the opening "For," rather than as a little pickup leading to "us," the more important word in that sentence. Well, nobody's perfect. And besides, he was writing in a hurry to meet the deadline of the looming debut performance. I've done some of my best writing on deadline. But then again, also some of my barely mediocre. And other than that awkward word stress, *For unto us* is a perfectly fine chorus.

Christine's soprano, Janet deBoer, got to do some of her bits about the shepherds abiding in the field (and washing their socks by night, as we like to joke), leading up to the chorus *Glory to God.* Running short on rehearsal time, we jumped ahead to that notorious *His yoke is easy*, which was going to require work. We made a good stab at it and decided to end the night, just for fun, with Christine taking us through the *Hallelujah* chorus. The choir loved it. Christine did too.

Rehearsal done, the singers made their way back to MacMillan Hall. There was the usual mild confusion of people milling around at the cubbyholes to put away their music and at the entryway cloakroom to put on their coats and boots. Christine was trying to wrangle her choristers to get them back on the bus for the trip home.

"Anyone feel like going for a beer?" asked a voice above the din. Probably one of my tenors. "We could go to Clancy's. It's not too far a walk."

"Some of us have to work in the morning," another voice said, prompting a few mild laughs.

"It's way too late," said someone else. "I have to get my beauty sleep."

More good-natured laughing.

"OK," said the first voice – who now I could see was indeed my tenor Bill. "What about tomorrow night, Friday? We could meet up around 7? Grayston, do you want to join us?"

"That sounds like fun," I could hear Marcie say. "Gray and I will join you tomorrow night."

"I'll join you too," said Christine's bass soloist, Gerry. "I'll try to persuade some of the others from our choir to come along. We'll talk about it on the bus, organize a carpool."

"Sounds like a plan, thanks," Gray said. "See you tomorrow night, whoever's coming."

"OK, St. Andrew's people," Christine said, raising her voice above the general hubbub. "Let's get on the bus. I'm sure we're all tired and want to get home. I know I do."

Chapter 17

Relieve thou the sorrows of my heart:
O bring thou me out of my troubles.

– Ps. 25, v. 17

Dogwalked, kayaked and breakfasted, I was perched on a stool at my kitchen counter enjoying a proper cup of tea – my own blend, made in my trusty old brown betty teapot though – *pace*, my old gran – poured into a big, sturdy ceramic mug, not a fine china teacup. I was contemplating a relaxing Friday after another successful choir practice.

Sometimes I do miss the buzz of the old newsroom. But there's also something to be said for a nice, relaxing morning. I'd gone far too many years with not enough of those.

Dun-dun. My cellphone telling me I had a text message.

It was Christine saying she wouldn't make the choir pub night tonight, though a few of her singers were making the trip.

Nice to see our two choirs bonding in their free time, I thought.

Dun-dun. "*u planning 2 go?*"

"*not sure*," I texted.

Dun-dun. "*well have fun if u do go*," she replied. "*say hi 2 ppl 4 me*."

"*OK*," I texted back.

Text speak, where brevity is a virtue if not also a necessity, is not unlike the rough-and-ready shorthand journalists have been using for decades in notes to ourselves and each other: "Lede" for the lead of a story, "follo" for a followup story, "graf" for paragraph. "TK" as a placeholder, "sked" for schedule. And so on. And of course "-30-" to signify "the end," the exact nature of its origin shrouded in mystery and still the subject of much debate.

Of course speech-to-text and autocorrect have removed much of the need for all that when texting. But obviously Christine, like me, is still used to typing sted (see what I did there?) of dictating. Like so much else in my little world, we're a dying breed.

Did I want to go to the pub tonight? Not really, I thought. I don't drink, so there's no appeal there. I like my singers well enough. And maybe it would be good to spend some time with them relaxing rather than rehearsing.

But truth be told, I'm still not feeling very sociable. It took a long time for me to even consider seeing another woman after my wife's death. But eventually I did, dating Priya briefly.

But then Priya died too.

Maybe the God I don't believe in really *does* exist. And maybe God just doesn't want me to be happy. Well, happier and in a relationship. Or maybe I'm just unlucky. What is it Yeats says?

Never give all the heart, for love
Will hardly seem worth thinking of
To passionate women if it seem
Certain, and they never dream
That it fades out from kiss to kiss;
For everything that's lovely is
But a brief, dreamy, kind delight.

And then he finishes with the gut punch:

He that made this knows all the cost,
For he gave all his heart and lost.

Oof. And the kids think Taylor Swift is the only one who can write about heartbreak.

Yeats knew whereof he speaks, at least twice having been hopelessly in love with the wrong woman. Way back in my freshman year, a few lifetimes ago, I had as an English Lit. Intro. prof a grad student not much older than we undergrads were. And he clearly did not appreciate having to teach this class. Toward the end of the final term, he gave us his brief lecture on William Butler Yeats. A few decades later, I can still remember it, word for word:

"OK, today we're doing Yeats," he said, walking to the front of the small lecture hall. "Yeats was a jerk. There are a couple of poems in the book. You should read them. They might be on the exam. OK, now we're doing Eliot…"

That's it. That was his entire lecture on Yeats. (We got a bit more detail on Eliot.) Now, to be fair, in many ways Yeats *was* a jerk. As a young man he fell madly in love with a woman named Maud Gonne. He proposed to her, but she spurned him and married someone else (a man Yeats called in one of his poems, just to spite him, "an old bellows full of angry wind"). When that man died, Yeats proposed to her again and she turned him down again.

All of this had inspired him to write some beautiful and heartfelt love poetry, including *Never give all the heart.*

So far, so sad, you might say. But here's where it gets creepy: Along the way, Yeats had also become infatuated with Maud Gonne's daughter, Iseult, and had even written some poems to her. And so Yeats also proposed to Iseult, who was almost 30 years younger than Yeats. She turned him down too. Yeats later married someone else and they had two kids and by most accounts were generally happy. I'm not sure what Mrs. Yeats thought about all this Maude and Iseult Gonne stuff.

So, OK, sure. Yeats was a jerk. But he also wrote some wonderful poetry. Maybe it's better to let a freshman class, most of whom have never heard of Yeats, discover his poetry first. Leave the weird lifestyle stuff for upper years. Maybe a senior seminar course?

Though as I get older myself, I think maybe not. Maybe by college, even in high school or before, we should be teaching our students the critical thinking skills they need to try to separate the artist from the art. We're none of us perfect, after all. Most of us are a complicated mixture of good and bad, noble and selfish. Maybe the sooner we learn that about ourselves and others, the better.

None of which answered the question of whether I wanted to go to the pub later tonight. After my second mug of tea, I decided I would go after all. If nothing else, it would give me some time to get to know Grayston Bergdorf a little better.

Chapter 18

He bringeth forth the clouds from the ends of the world
and sendeth forth lightnings for the rain,
bringing the winds out of his treasuries.

– Ps. 135, v. 7

By afternoon it had started to rain. Glad I'd done my paddle first thing in the morning. Wolf took one look out the window and gave a small whine. So much for a long walk. Her husky genes make her nearly impervious to cold, her husky fur not so well suited to the wet.

It wasn't quite a downpour, but rain enough that you noticed it. Steady. Enough to darken the already grey Grayston sky. Another bit of poetry – centuries older than Yeats and one that inspired English composers Taverner, Tye and Sheppard – popped into my head:

Westron wynde when wyll thow blow
the smalle rayne downe can Rayne
Cryst yf my love were in my Armys
And I yn my bed Agayne.

We often forget how racy the 16th century actually was. Maybe I could sneak one of their *Westron Wynde* masses into a service sometime. Just don't tell the congregation what the sacred music is based on. They'd fire me for sure.

The rain made it a good day to stay inside and putter. Do the dishes. A little reading. A bit of piano, just to keep the fingers – and mind – nimble. Played through a few of the easy (well, easier) Bach two-part and three-part inventions. Always soothing to see the great master fully in control of his resources.

I miss having a proper upright piano (could never afford a grand, even a baby grand). But my electronic keyboard has all 88 keys and still I can pick it up and carry it under my arm. Try doing that with a real piano. Besides, it never goes out of tune – in fact, I can adjust the tuning to A415 Baroque pitch if I want to. I can also make it sound like a harpsichord, organ or even honky-tonk. And it has a volume control, so as not to disturb my condo neighbors. To be completely quiet, I can even plug in headphones.

Maybe progress ain't always so bad after all.

The rain let up enough after dinner that Wolf – reluctantly – agreed to a walk sufficient only to do her business before tugging me back in the direction of home. I dried her off and changed out of my muddy dogwalking duds into some semi-decent clothes. Remembering to bring an umbrella (whether I'd remember to bring it home with me was another story), I headed off to Clancy's to join with whatever choristers had braved the weather to meet there.

It was time to be social.

My timing was excellent. Or maybe just lucky. I arrived at Clancy's, a bar that fancies itself an Irish pub, just as the sky opened up with another heavy downpour. The heavens were telling me to get inside quickly.

By this time it was past 8 and the gathering was in full swing. About a dozen members from the combined choirs had commandeered the back corner, pushing together a few tables to accommodate everyone. Shaking my umbrella and hanging it on a hook with my coat, I went over to join the crowd.

By most bar standards they weren't a particularly raucous group. But a few choristers were clearly a couple of beers ahead of the game and the various simultaneous conversations were lively and cheerful. I hoped the Alliston crowd had designated drivers.

I was able to squeeze in across from Gray and Marcie, who greeted me with happy smiles.

"Glad you could make it, Mr. Heywood," Marcie said.

"Thanks. And you know you can call me Dugan."

"I was telling Marcie how well I think the choir is doing," Gray said.

"Nice of you to say."

"The other altos have been very welcoming," Gray said. "I'm quite happy to sit in on the choruses to help out if, if that's OK with you."

"Yes, that would be great," I said. "The other soloists will be doing the same. It'll take some choreography to get you all in and out for your solos. But I think we can make it work."

"I was glad I had a chance to speak with that girl – young woman – Cassie from the other choir," Gray said. "She asked me a bit about what it's like to be a 'famous' singer. I told her I wasn't that famous yet. But maybe one day I would be."

Marcie took his hand and they shared a smile.

"I told her the worst part was all the running around, the touring. And the best part was of course the music. And getting to sing with other good musicians."

"She did seem quite taken with you," Marcie said, teasingly.

"She told me she'd auditioned for the alto solos but didn't make the cut. I encouraged her to keep at it and try again next time."

"And then her mother came and yanked her away," I said. "She didn't seem very happy with you."

"That she was not," Gray said. "I've no idea why. I heard her say something like, 'You'd better hope your father doesn't hear about this' as she hauled Cassie away."

Chapter 19

This poor man cried, and the Lord heard him;
yea, and saved him out of all his troubles.

– Ps. 34, v. 6

On Saturdays the bar has live music – usually some local kids with a garage band dreaming of rock stardom – but others nights it's just canned music. Between that and all the talking, it was hard to hold a conversation amid the noise. Another reason I don't often go to bars.

"Mr. Heywood. Dugan," Marcie said. "I've been meaning to ask you something."

"Sure. What?"

"Don't most choirs do *Messiah* at Christmas?"

"True."

"I mean, the choir at St. Nicholas has done it almost every year. And always at Christmas. I've been going to those since I was a little girl."

"So *that's* why you know it so well," I teased. St. Nick's had always been a men-and-boys choir. Until the recent scandal. So Marcie wouldn't have been able to sing with them until now. But listening to it every year is a good way to learn it too.

"So why are we doing it in spring?" she asked. "Just to avoid conflicting with them?"

"I guess that's part of it," I said. "Although the new music director there has agreed to be more co-operative with other choirs in Grayston and beyond. Share the wealth, as it were."

"But it does have a nice historical ring to it too," Gray said.

I smiled.

"What do you mean?" Marcie asked.

Grayston Bergdorf looked over at me. I gave a small nod. I was pretty sure I knew what he was going to say. It's a good story. I'd let him tell it.

"Not long after he wrote it," Gray said, settling in to his tale, "Handel produced and conducted many performances of *Messiah*. In London. At Christmastime. And they got bigger and bigger. Most of them were benefits for an orphanage."

"*Messiah* has a long history of being a fundraiser," I said.

Gray smiled, ready to continue with the story. It was like we were a couple of old vaudeville guys sharing the stage in a duo act.

"Right," Gray said. "But the *first* performance of *Messiah* wasn't at Christmas. And it wasn't even in London."

"Why not?" Marcie asked.

"Despite his many successes over the years," Gray said. "Handel also struggled. Went bankrupt twice. Even in a good year he was always having money troubles. Like most of us musicians. Same as today."

Don't I know it, I thought.

Our server came by asking about more rounds. By the looks of it, Gray and Marcie had had one beer each and declined a refill. I decided to go for another cranberry juice. What the hell. Live it up a little.

"Handel had been writing operas for London," Gray said, picking up the story again. "But it was always an up-and-down thing. Operas can take a long time to write, even for Handel. And they're expensive to put on. And not always popular."

"Then there's MacSwiney," I said, to grease the wheels.

Gray chuckled. "Ya, there's that."

"Who's that?" Marcie asked. Clearly, she was enjoying her boyfriend telling the story as much as he was having fun telling it.

"Right," he said. "We're talking some years' difference. But among the occasional flops and successes, it didn't help that in 1713, Handel's theatre manager – Owen Swiney, or MacSwiney, depending on whom he was trying to swindle at the time – ran off with all the money from one of Handel's operas. It took Handel quite a while to recover from that loss.

"So by 1742, after some other losses and disappointments, Handel had pretty much given up on opera. Someone in Dublin offered to pay him for a new work and Handel was happy to oblige. He needed the money. Wrote *Messiah* in just about three weeks – most of it on the sea voyage from London to Dublin."

"Neat," Marcie said. "I didn't know that."

"Not many other than music nerds do," I said.

"But why *Messiah*?" Marcie asked.

"Like I said, operas can take a long time to write," Gray said, "and they're expensive to produce. Handel needed money fast. And an oratorio doesn't need sets or costumes or staging."

"It's like opera on the radio," Marcie joked. "Or a podcast."

"Exactly."

Gray took the last swallow of his beer.

"But there was another reason," he said, smiling over at me, knowing we shared another bit of trivia.

"It was Lent, like we're in now," he said. "And in one of its periodic crackdowns, the church had forbidden opera performances during Lent. It was another one of the reasons why Handel often had money troubles – that's 40 days when all the theatres were dark. Hard to make money if there's no audience. *Messiah* shares pretty much the same format as an opera – recits, solo arias, a few choruses, all telling a narrative story. But by performing it as an oratorio – without any acting or staging – Handel had found a loophole."

"But even then they weren't allowed to perform it in a church," I said, wrapping up my part of our vaudeville act. "That first Dublin performance was in a big hall instead."

"Wait a minute," Marcie said. "I just thought of something."

We both looked at her, wondering what she would say.

"You know Leonard Cohen, the Canadian songwriter."

We nodded. Even *I* know who Leonard Cohen is.

"Late in his career, his manager stole all his money too," Marcie said. "It left him broke. He pretty much had to come out of retirement and go back on the road to try to earn his money back."

"I heard about that," Gray said. "His manager even went to jail over it."

"Unlike MacSwiney," I said, "though Cohen's manager never did pay him back."

"Cohen revived one of his old songs," Marcie said. "It hadn't done very well at first, though it became popular with some covers and a movie tie-in. But whatever money that had made him got wiped out by the thief. Luckily it became a big hit for him the second time around."

"Your point being?" I asked, though I thought I knew where she was going with it.

Marcie smiled, justly proud of herself.

"I just think it's cool that, a couple of centuries apart, Handel's *Hallelujah* and Leonard Cohen's *Hallelujah* helped bring each of them back from the brink of bankruptcy."

Chapter 20

Look upon the covenant, for the dark places of the earth are full of the habitations of cruelty.

– Ps. 74, v. 20

I had some halting conversations with a few others around the table. But most of them were too far away and it was too loud for any sort of meaningful exchange. I decided to pack it in and go home. I could always use Wolf as my excuse.

As I stood up to take my leave, a few others joined me. Maybe they have dogs too. Gray and Marcie also decided to leave. Thankfully our server had kept the bills separate, so paying didn't take very long. My two cranberry juices didn't break the bank, but it probably would have been cheaper to order a beer. The hidden cost of being abstemious. We huddled by the coat hooks figuring out whose was whose. I found my coat and even remembered my umbrella.

As we stepped outside, the side street that houses Clancy's seemed wonderfully quiet compared to the noise inside the bar. Five of us – two couples and loner me as usual – were chatting politely before saying goodbye and going our separate ways.

The rain had reduced to what my old gran would probably call a 'Scotch mist.' Barely a sprinkle, but more than enough to darken the already dark night sky – all those millions of little raindrops each a tiny prism scattering the meagre available light.

Reaching out to take Marcie's hand, Grayston Bergdorf stepped off the curb onto the street still slick from the rain. I became aware of a noise and some movement to my left.

A large dark vehicle, no headlights, was racing toward us, going way too fast and weaving erratically.

Marcie screamed Gray's name in warning. But instead of looking to his left at the oncoming vehicle, he instinctively looked back at his girlfriend to see what she wanted.

There was an awful thud. And then a squeal of tires as the vehicle – whatever it was – turned the corner and sped away. I tried to catch the licence plate but couldn't.

"Call 911!" Marcie shouted, bending down. Gray lay sprawled on the pavement, not moving.

One of the other singers already had her phone out and was calling 911. In barely a moment I could hear the sound of an approaching siren. We were only a few blocks from the hospital. Sometimes living in a small town is a blessing.

In a few minutes the ambulance came. Soon the paramedics had assessed Gray, lifted him carefully onto a gurney and whisked him away, Marcie, white-faced and shaken, riding in the back with him and holding his hand. A police car had arrived only a few moments after the ambulance, an encouraging sign that our 911 service was operating efficiently.

I recognized the cop as he got out of his car. He and I were not exactly friends, but I'd dealt with him before and we had what you might call a grudging respect for each other.

"Officer Kang," I said.

"Mr. Heywood," he replied, taking out a pad and pen. "I gather there's been an accident. Were you here when it happened?"

"A few of us were," I said, gesturing vaguely to the other two who remained now that Gray and Marcie had gone.

"Good evening," he said to them. "My name is Officer Liu Kang with the Grayston police department. "I'm sorry you've had what's probably been an upsetting experience. But it's important that we get all the facts while they're still fresh in your minds.

"I'm going to have to ask you some questions and take some notes. Later on, I'd like you to come to the station for a formal statement."

I had to give Kang credit. Though he's always been a bit cool and aloof with me, he seemed genuinely caring and respectful of the two young women standing there, who did indeed look shocked and confused. In my years at the paper I'd seen more than my share of car accidents, fires and other tragedies. It tends to harden you. It has to, or otherwise you wouldn't be able to do the job.

But I could feel it too. Another goddamn drunk driver. Like the one who'd killed my wife and daughter. Stupid bastard. I felt a pain well up that I hadn't felt in a long time and struggled to tamp it down. I wouldn't do anyone any good by falling apart. I tried to concentrate on remembering what I'd seen and heard. Being useful helps keep the grief at bay.

First, Kang got their names and addresses. One was an alto in my choir. The other was a soprano from the Alliston choir whom I recognized but didn't know. Evidently they were already friends from before our joint project.

"Who called 911?" Kang asked.

"I did," said Elaine, the alto from my choir. Like me, she was struggling to keep it together.

"Thank you for being so quick with that," Kang said.

"Sometimes even a few minutes can make a big difference in an accident like this."

"Is he going to be OK?" the other woman asked.

"I'm afraid I don't know," Kang said. "We'll have to leave that to the doctors and nurses. But I'm sure they're doing their best."

I was glad to see Kang handling things with tact and care. I'd have to remember to thank him for that.

In short order, Kang had spoken to each of us, taking our ID and a brief statement that we'd elaborate on later.

Unfortunately, there wasn't much to go on.

It had all happened so fast, the three of us agreed. (I'm not sure Marcie would have much to add either. Nor Gray, when they had a chance to ask him.) We were standing talking, Gray had stepped off the curb. I was pretty sure – but not absolutely – he'd even instinctively looked for any traffic before he did. The vehicle seemed to have come out of nowhere and without warning. And at terrific speed. None of us remembered hearing a car horn. Just the sound of the thud as it hit his body.

But this is where it got hazy. Even we three eyewitnesses couldn't agree on what the vehicle looked like. We all agreed it was big. I thought it was black and probably an SUV. Elaine agreed it was probably some kind of SUV, but might have been dark blue or even dark grey. The cloudy night and the dim street lighting made it hard to tell. The other singer, whose name was Angie, agreed with me that it was probably black, but might have been a sedan instead of an SUV.

I was reminded why the police and courts have a hard time relying on eyewitness testimony.

Kang thanked us for our time and told us we should come down to the station soon to confirm our statements.

"And if you remember anything else in the meantime," he said, giving each of us his business card, "please don't hesitate to call me."

Chapter 21

Surely thou hast seen it; for thou beholdest trouble and sorrow, that thou mayest take the matter into thy hand.

– Ps. 10, v. 15

As Kang walked back to his cruiser, I saw a familiar face. Sandra Novak had been standing there for a while, hanging back to let Kang do his thing before speaking to us. She must have heard the 911 call on the *Gazette's* police scanner. The newsroom is only a few blocks away from the pub – convenient as one of the spots where reporters and deskers sometimes gather after work if they want something stronger than Maggie's coffee.

So it was a short walk. Sandra must have drawn the weekend shift since last I saw her for breakfast.

"Hey, Dugan," she said, stepping forward and nodding to me.

"Good evening, ladies," she continued. "I'm Sandra Novak from the *Grayston Gazette*. I know you've had a bit of a difficult experience. But, as the officer said, it's important that you speak about it while it's fresh in your minds."

The women nodded. Kang's manner – and a bit of time – had managed to wear off some of the shock. Though that was an illusion. I know from experience that this was probably just a brief lull. More than anything they were numb. The full effect of seeing a tragedy like that wouldn't really hit them til later. Trust me, I know.

"Without jumping too much to a conclusion," Sandra said, "this looks to have been a pretty simple hit-and-run accident. But I'm sure you can appreciate that we don't want bad drivers on the road. And we should all do our part to help the police in their investigation. So what can you tell me?"

I let Sandra speak to the women, get some information and maybe a few quotes from them for any story she might write. It might be nothing more than a brief squib, a little story for the website and maybe the print edition if there was room. But you never know. It might provide material for some later feature, maybe a bigger investigation into traffic accidents and road safety.

Sandra concentrated on the women. She knew she could get anything she needed from me later.

Elaine and Angie repeated what they'd told Kang. Which wasn't much. A vehicle – maybe an SUV, maybe a car. And dark – maybe black, or some other color. It came out of nowhere and drove away fast. They weren't sure it had even slowed down after hitting Gray and then speeding off.

Like Kang, Sandra got their names and numbers and left each with her business card, asking them to call if they had any information to add.

With that, they walked slowly away, hugging each other. Angie had her head tilted on Elaine's shoulder. It looked like both of them were crying. There'd be more of that later too.

"How about you?" Sandra asked, turning to me. "Anything to add?"

"Not really," I said. "I'm leaning toward a black SUV. But I can't be sure either."

"It's like grey cats," Sandra said. "They all look the same in the dark."

"I don't remember seeing any headlights," I said. "Nor hearing a horn before Gray got hit. And when the car – SUV, whatever it was – sped off, I couldn't see the back plate."

"So we're thinking drunk driver?"

"That's what it looks like at first glance," I said. "But you and I have had the same editors drill it into us: 'Don't make any assumptions.'"

"Ya, well. I'm going to pop over to the hospital and check on –" Sandra checked the name in her notepad "– Grayston Bergdorf. And if Kang's not there I can get him by phone. Then I should write something up. I'm sorry about your friend."

"Thanks. When you get to the hospital, give me a call or text, let me know how he is."

"Will do."

"Thanks."

"Seeya later."

I walked home in a daze. Dogs are sensitive. When I got in the door, Wolf could tell I was upset about something. She cocked her head at me and gave a small whine. On autopilot, I took her for a final pee before bed, cut short because the rain had started up again. I was glad it hadn't been raining much on my walk home. We got back inside, only slightly wet. Wolf got in the door and gave a big shake, leaving her drier and me wetter. Sometimes I wish I could do that too.

There was a message on my cellphone. From Sandra.

She wasn't allowed to see him, but nurses told her Gray had a broken leg, a damaged knee and some pretty severe bruising. He was also still unconscious.

Sandra had spoken by phone with Kang and had gotten a brief quote from Marcie. But Marcie was still pretty upset. Sandra said Marcie had wanted to stay with Gray overnight.

But since she wasn't family, the hospital had sent her home.

I'd call her tomorrow to see how she was doing. Poor kid. It must have been tough.

Chapter 22

O my God, I cry in the daytime, but thou hearest not;
and in the night-season also I take no rest.

– Ps. 22, v. 2

I was tired but too wound up to go to sleep. I went to bed but when I closed my eyes, my mind filled with a jumble of images, real and imagined. They played like a movie in my head: Jeri in the car driving back from the cabin, Chelsea in the baby seat in the back. A pickup truck weaving and smashing into them, pushing them off the road and into the swampy water beside it. The pickup truck – in this fevered scenario a black one – became a black SUV slamming into Gray Bergdorf.

I opened my eyes – I hadn't ever really been asleep – got up and got dressed again. Snuggled in a blanket in her crate with the door open, Wolf – sleeping happily – roused just enough to look my way, decide I was in no immediate danger and calmly put her head back down. Sleeping the sleep of the just.

Back in the kitchen, I made tea and stayed up late, trying to think about Gray Bergdorf instead of my lovely dead family. It was hard to get the image of him sprawled on the pavement out of my mind. But at least better than my personal alternative. I tried to review the events in my mind, but got no further ahead.

A black SUV (probably). No headlights. Comes out of nowhere, weaving and driving fast. No horn. Hits Gray. Doesn't stop. Speeds off around the corner. Can't see a licence plate.

That's it.

I texted Sandra: "*any record of similar hit-and-runs?*"

Dun-dun: "*way ahead of u sherlock. already looking into that. will let u know. breakfast monday?*"

"*u bet*," I texted back. "*cu then*"

Can't sleep? When in doubt, walk the dog. I know the adage, 'Let sleeping dogs lie.' (Never say 'old adage,' my inner editor voice reminded me – that's redundant.) But though Wolf was happily curled up and snoozing, she seemed equally happy to hear me say "walk?" and "park?" She jumped to her feet, tail wagging.

The on-again-off-again rain had let up again, so I risked leaving the umbrella behind and changed into my dogwalking duds. It was warm enough that a lighter rain jacket worked – but I put on rubber boots just to be safe. The grass would be squishy.

The Grandview sits nearly kitty-corner from the main city park, which covers an area of maybe four city blocks. Around the corner at the edge of the park stands a bit of Grayston's 19th-century history. The city has preserved one gaslamp – the last reminder of many dozens that once lit up the oldest part of town. Even after more than a century, the utility company has kept the flame lit. I like to think of it as our very own little bit of Sherlockiana.

It's been a bone of contention over the years, since city funds subsidize the cost of maintaining it and keeping the flame lit. Every few years, some tightwad city councillor moans about the cost and eyes it as a line item on the city budget. And every time, most of the other councillors have to remind the misguided penny pincher that not only is it a valuable piece of local history, but also it more than pays for itself as a tourist attraction.

I can vouch for that. Lots of the tourist looky-loos who come to check out the Grandview for its reputation as a swanky Jazz Age hotel also go around the corner to take a selfie standing under the last gaslamp.

The old courthouse, which once also held the police station and a small jail til the cop shop moved to bigger and newer digs as the town grew, sits at the top end of the park facing the lake to the south, a solid limestone building bespeaking order and probity. The courts are in the new cop shop too, so I'm not sure what function the old courthouse now serves. Maybe just storage. There was some talk of turning it into a town museum, but city council has never yet scraped up the funding.

Late at night (well, early morning) its impressive central dome – greened copper, like that of city hall but smaller and also like the spire of St. Nicholas – looms over the park as a reminder and warning to be good, law-abiding citizens. Which nowadays mostly tells students not to get caught drinking in public and dog walkers like me to pick up their poop.

At this hour, Wolf and I had the big park almost all to ourselves. I could see one couple holding hands and walking back toward campus. Up to my right, I could see just a bit of the steeple of St. Quentin's – which reminded me I should spend some of my Saturday going over the music for Sunday. Practice makes perfect. But only if you practise perfectly. My organ work was still rudimentary at best and required regular maintenance. No point giving my detractors more reason to replace me.

Maybe I shouldn't be so worried. Even the great J.S. Bach got his job at Leipzig only as third choice, after Telemann and some other guy whose name history and I don't remember had each turned it down. Some wag on the Leipzig town council said "since the best man could not be obtained, mediocre ones would have to be accepted." But what did *he* know?

Because it was late and there might be skunks or other critters lurking about, I kept Wolf on her leash, walking slowly and giving her lots of chance to sniff around and explore. This was her time more than mine. But, like kayaking, walking also gave me time to think and my mind to wander even more than my feet.

I couldn't stop thinking about the accident. Assuming that's what it was. It probably was. Just some stupid drunk driver – another redundant phrase, driving drunk being by definition stupid. Maybe even someone who'd been somewhere else in the bar with us. I don't remember noticing anyone particularly loud or aggressive. Our little party of singers was lively, but not nearly as boisterous as the crowd over in the other corner watching a game on TV. Besides, sometimes it's the quiet, moody drunks you have to watch out for. And bartenders are pretty responsible about cutting someone off if they look like they've had too much. Even taking away their keys and making them call a cab.

I'd have to mention that to Sandra on Monday, that she should check with the bar staff. She'd probably thought of that already. No flies on her. But Clancy's is not the only bar downtown. And they all tend to be pretty busy come the weekend. The students especially like to blow off steam. So that driver could have come from anywhere. Maybe the cops would have reports of a similar vehicle involved in alcohol-related stops or accidents. It would help if we could nail down the vehicle description.

But why should I get involved? It would only dredge up more painful memories for me. Sure, I had a personal stake because Gray had become a friend of sorts, as was his girlfriend, and I was there when it happened. But other than giving my statement to the police – another thing I needed to do on Saturday, as well as check in on Marcie – there was nothing I could do about it. And no need. The cops had their investigating to do. And I was sure Sandra would keep tabs on the story and any developments. If there were any to find.

I should just stay in my lane.

Chapter 23

But lo, thou requirest truth in the inward parts
and shalt make me to understand wisdom secretly.

– Ps. 51, v. 6

The usual morning stuff out of the way, I was once again stooled at my kitchen counter over a mug of tea, thinking about how to structure my day. Tired from her walk, Wolf was once again asleep on the floor in front the fireplace. No fire, though. The weather was already warming up enough that it wasn't really necessary. Maybe tonight, just for the ambiance.

First I put a call in to Marcie. Straight to voicemail, so either she had her phone off or was already talking to someone. I left a message, hoping she was OK and saying I'd understand if she wanted to skip church in the morning. "You do whatever feels best for you," I told the recording. "And for Gray too. Take care."

It was time to give Kang my formal witness statement on Gray's accident. I wished I had more detail to add. But nothing new had come to mind. Maybe the others had come up with something since last night. Let's hope. The police didn't have much to go on.

I checked the *Gazette* website to see what Sandra had filed. It wasn't much either:

Police seek help
in hit-and-run

The story with it – just a one-graf squib, no byline –

didn't even mention Gray by name. He was just "a man" who "sustained injuries" around 10 p.m. on Friday night in front of Clancy's bar. Police were seeking information on a "dark vehicle" seen in the vicinity at the time.

Not just in brevity but in form, Sandra had crafted it carefully to avoid any possible legal blowback and in a deliberate effort not to taint any other witness statements. The implication, of course, was that the vehicle had struck and injured the man and did not remain at the scene. The squib, brief as it was, could just have said that. Most readers would take it that way anyway. But, as they say in *Perry Mason* and so many other of those TV courtroom scenes, it's important not to "lead the witness."

As journalists, we're taught to be careful in our phrasing. Unless we know information to be true, we're not supposed to jump to conclusions. So, absent established facts – when reporting on an accident, for instance – you're not supposed to write that Vehicle A struck Vehicle B. That's for police and the courts to determine. And maybe also an insurance investigator. So, at least in the first reports of the story, good editors drill into us to write that Vehicle A and Vehicle B were "in collision." This avoids us, the media, assigning fault or blame.

It ends up sounding a bit stilted or awkward. Even silly. But don't shoot the messenger. Blame the lawyers.

It's one of my issues, frankly, with the internet in general and so-called "citizen journalism" in particular. It's the amateurs. As a longtime professional journalist who takes the profession seriously, I have mixed feelings. Yes, on the one hand, professional journalists have a long history of often relying on whistleblowers and other inside sources

– civilians, laypeople, non-journalists, whatever you want to call them – to provide us with information we might not otherwise easily obtain. If at all. Think Watergate and Deep Throat – or other more recent examples.

But Woodward and Bernstein were themselves pros who knew how to take those tips from Deep Throat not just at face value but as pieces of a larger investigative puzzle. They didn't just blab what Deep Throat had told them – the nub of which was, after all, the fairly obvious advice to "follow the money." Deep Throat really just helped them confirm some of what they already knew. Or suspected.

Of course it also helped that *they* knew – though they kept this secret, respecting their source – that Deep Throat was well placed to be giving them an accurate inside scoop. He wasn't just some crank with an ax to grind.

And that's my problem with today, where the internet, social media and personal blogs give just about anybody the ability to say – to 'publish' – whatever they want whenever they want. Libel? Defamation? Who cares? Lawyers? Who needs 'em? Facts? Pfft! People, they think, should have a 'right' to say whatever they want.

Obviously some – even many – of these internet warriors are doing good work, serving a good cause. Especially as 'legacy media' get increasingly bogged down and even stifled by big-money interests. When the *Gazette*, under its former private owner, bravely took up the Gascoyne scandal, the publisher took his paper way out on a limb, risking the loss of both readers and advertisers for the sake of exposing a harsh and harmful truth. Would the paper's current corporate owners – Blackwell Holdings and the hedge funds and shareholders who control it – take such a principled risk today? I doubt it. (Though to be fair, Blackwell *did* run some of the later follo stories in the aftermath. But by then the truth of the stories had been established. And truth is a valid defence in defamation.)

My real problem is with the minority of bloggers and social media blowhards who trade in harmful rumor, even outright falsehood, merely in pursuit of clicks and 'influence' – and who sneer at 'gatekeepers.' Well, in my opinion sometimes you need gatekeepers to weed out the riffraff and stomp on the bullshit. There's a reason bars often have bouncers.

Which reminded me again I should touch base with Sandra about our bar and any others from Friday night.

Chapter 24

Let me not be disappointed of my hope.

– Ps. 119, v. 115

The weather had cleared. And warmed up enough that my walk over to the police station was pleasant, if still a bit cool. Pretty soon the flowers would start to appear and the trees to bud. There's a reason the church sees Easter as a time of rebirth and resurrection. It is, after all, tied to the vernal equinox, in the same way that Christmas is tied to the winter solstice – a birth of a different kind. It's always puzzled me that the church has never made as big a deal, festival-wise, of either the summer solstice or the autumnal equinox. I wonder why? I should look into that, just for fun.

When I got to the cop shop – a building decades newer than the old courthouse but already beginning to show its age and signs of wear – the front desk told me Liu Kang was off shift. And so was my old cop friend Don Patterson. So I told the officer at the desk why I was there and he found another officer to take my statement.

That officer – a young woman who reminded me a bit of Priya – led me to a small interview room to take my statement. Her name tag said Chaidee. She took notes by hand, excused herself briefly and returned with a computer printout. I read over the narrative – her notes were accurate, she'd make a good reporter – and signed at the bottom.

Sadly, what I could offer was still pretty scant.

I asked about the other witnesses and she confirmed that Elaine and Angie had come in together first thing in the morning to give their own statements. Kang had taken Marcie's last night at the hospital. Gray Bergdorf was still unconscious. We weren't much farther ahead.

The only speck of good news seemed to be that the four of us now agreed the vehicle that struck Gray was a dark SUV, though there was still some dispute as to the color. And even after looking at pictures of a whole bunch of them, none of us had been able to ID a make and model. They all look so similar. So much for the free market promoting choice and diversity.

I mentioned Sandra's web post and Chaidee said so far no other witnesses had come forward. But she remained hopeful.

"Sometimes it takes people a while to remember what they saw," she said. "Or they don't think they have anything to add. And others just don't like talking to the police."

"Occupational hazard," I said. "Same for journalists sometimes."

She gave a small smile, maybe even a teasing grin.

"Besides," she said, "not everyone reads the *Gazette*, you know."

"Don't I know it," I said, smiling back.

Duty called. I left Officer Chaidee to her paperwork. I walked back to the main drag and then upstreet – as we say in Grayston – from the cop shop toward St. Quentin's and my beckoning organ bench. Time to pull out all the stops. Or at least some of them.

Once at the church, I traded my street shoes for my special organ shoes – actually dancer's shoes I had to order from a theatrical supply house. They have a leather sole and toes more pointy than I normally like, but that makes them work better for the organ pedals, where you need to be nimble.

Before taking up St. Quentin's I'd spent some years as an occasional organist on call for various churches around town – mostly regardless of denomination – filling in for fellow musicians who fell sick or just wanted a holiday. This was good for keeping me in practice (and brought in a little money on the side), but also often presented a challenge.

Unlike most instrumentalists – your flutist, your violinist, your trumpeter – an organist can't exactly take the instrument along. You're at the mercy of whatever instrument they hand you. It's pretty much the same for piano players – unless you're like that wonderfully eccentric and brilliant Canadian pianist Glenn Gould, who almost always brought his beloved Steinway CD 318 with him for concerts and later, when he abandoned the concert hall, for recording sessions.

But there's a saving grace, of sorts: The American Guild of Organists. To make life a little easier, and to prevent organists from tearing out their hair, the AGO – God love 'em – has decreed a standard layout for keyboards and, more important, for all the many stops and buttons and levers that make a church organ look at bit like the instrument panel on the flight deck of a passenger jet. So although each organ still tends to have its own little quirks, at least when you parachute in to help out, as I often had done, you can rest easy that the layout and configuration will be more or less the same from place to place.

Thank goodness for small mercies.

The St. Q organ is fairly simple as church organs go: two keyboards, called manuals, stacked at an angle one atop the other, and a pedal board spanning the AGO-standard two and a half octaves. Plus enough stops to pull and buttons to push to make driving a car seem so much easier.

I ran through the hymns and anthem for Sunday – nothing difficult but sadly also nothing to make the heart melt. Easter would come soon with some better ones. At the piano in the hall – a Steinway, though not of course Gould's – I went back over some bits of *Messiah*, noting passages that still needed work and attention. We were coming along, but still had a ways to go.

Which made me think of Gray. I should phone the hospital and check up on him. I was also counting on Sandra to update me on any major developments, good or bad.

I was a little surprised to see Marcie at church the next morning. But people deal with stress in different ways. Clearly Marcie had decided she'd rather be among friends and singing than sitting at home – or maybe worse, at Gray's hospital bedside – moping and worrying.

I told her I was glad to see her and said again how sorry I was about Gray. Marcie still looked a little shellshocked, but she managed a wan smile and a brave face. During the service I could hear her in the hymns – sometimes faltering, other times seeming to gain strength from the words. Hey, whatever works. I have my poetry – my Frost, my Yeats, my Shakespeare – others have their hymn book. Judge not lest ye be judged.

Marcie had several choir friends around her for support after the service, so I ducked out of coffee hour early and went home. Wolf was glad to be back in the park, even though the overnight rain had turned the ground, with the remaining scattered snow, into a slushy mess. Should have worn my rubber boots. The courthouse in the distance looking less ominous in the daylight diffused through the overcast sky. This time there were a few more dog people to nod at as we passed. But none of Wolf's friends, nor mine, so we didn't stop to talk.

Besides, it had started to rain. Again.

Chapter 25

O let me hear thy loving-kindness in the morning,
for in thee is my trust.

– Ps. 143, v. 8

Maggie's opens at 6, but because the newsroom night shift – known in lore as the "lobster shift" – ends at 7 (barring world war or some other major breaking news story), Sandra Novak and I had set our standing Monday breakfast date for 7.

Or 7-ish. If she's working lobster, Sandra arrives just a few minutes later – however much time it takes her to shut down her computer and walk down a couple of flights of stairs from the newsroom next door. I try to be on time or even a bit early, to set a good example. It's the reporter in me. And musician too.

I'd barely sat down at one of the twofer booths along the wall when Sandra joined me. It being early and not yet very busy, George Papadakis himself, the longtime owner, came over to take our orders. There hasn't been an actual Maggie for a couple of decades since she retired and George bought the world's best diner from her.

"Good morning, Senator," he said to me. "Ms. Senator," he said with a polite nod to Sandra. "We'll start with the usual?"

"Morning, George," we both replied in unison. Sandra beat me to the next line.

"That'd be great, thanks."

It's not like we're anyone special. For reasons no one's quite been able to figure out, George calls pretty much anyone and everyone "Senator." To the best of my knowledge and research, Grayston has never produced an actual senator. Maybe George thinks it's a generic term of respect.

I'll take it.

George went off to the kitchen at the back. Sandra was barely out of her coat when already he'd come back with a tray, placing down coffee in a thick china mug for her and tea for me in one of those little stainless-steel teapots, also with a mug. No fancy china cup and saucer at Maggie's, which suits me just fine.

Sandra loaded hers up with milk and sugar. I let my tea steep a bit longer. No milk or sugar for me. I drink it "clear," as we tea grannies say.

Since there's something to be said for tradition – and since Maggie's hadn't quite risen to the fanciful heights of Eggs Benedict at the trendy café Jentacular over the causeway bridge in the township – we ordered our usual breakfasts. Poached, bacon and brown toast for me, with extra tomatoes instead of homefries. Trying to cut down on carbs. Over easy, sausage, homefries and white toast for Sandra. There's no accounting for taste. Such a smart woman otherwise.

"How was work?"

"They keep dragging me back onto the desk," Sandra said, not happy about it.

"Isn't the pay a bit better?" I said. "Aren't the hours a little more regular?"

"Sure. But sometimes that means the dreaded night shift, like I'm on now."

"True."

"Besides," Sandra said. "I *like* reporting. I *like* writing. Well, not always the actual writing. But the investigating. The running around and asking people questions. Getting answers."

"You're naturally curious."

"Or naturally nosy." She grinned. "But seriously, I'm a people person. I don't like being chained to a desk hardly interacting with anyone except some other editor."

"You get to interact with reporters on their stories."

"The city and news editors do," she said. "As a copy editor, not so much. Besides, have you *met* reporters? They're not all charming like me, you know."

"I kinda liked being a copy editor," I said. "Trimming a story to just the right size. Not hacking it in half, but the careful pruning. Finding a way to say something in three words instead of five or six. Crafting the perfect hed. I found that satisfying."

"That's cuz you're more anal than I am," she said with a smirk. "I'm more of a big-picture gal."

George came back with our breakfasts. We took a pause to dig in for a few bites.

"So, Lois Lane," I said in a fit of originality, "what's news?"

"Oh, the usual. You want the national chicanery and corruption, or the local?"

"Local, please. The national I can get on TV."

Cherishing her mug in both hands, Sandra inhaled the coffee smell before taking a swig.

"Aside from the usual arguments over the city snow budget, before they put me on lobster for the week, Des and I are wrapping up our stories on Czardas and Magyar Developments. Des has been covering the business angle and I've been dealing with the court stuff. The trial starts in a couple of weeks."

Des was Des Hoffman, the paper's business reporter – and staff being short he also had other beats, which for all I knew included the town garden tour. The Czardas/Magyar stuff was a mess that had roped me in last year, as yet another ripple from the Gascoyne scandal continued to disturb the small pond that Grayston sometimes seems to be.

"Any news on that hit-and-run from Friday night?"

"A few things to pursue," Sandra said. "I can usually put in a few calls before my desking shift ends."

You know things are tight when you have reporters and copy editors overlapping and doing both jobs.

"By the way," she said, "what kind of name is Grayston? Is he from here?"

"No," I said, "he's not named for the town. That's just a coincidence. He doesn't even live here, but his girlfriend does. Her friends rag him about it all the time. He's named after another famous singer, Grayston Burgess."

"Never heard of him."

"Well, famous if you're into early music, particularly countertenors."

"Kind of a niche."

"True."

"But still," she said, teasingly, "it's no more weird than Dugan."

"Good Scots name," I said. "My given name is my mother's birth name. You know, just like Clark Kent."

"I guess that's why you became a newspaperman."

"Could be. Speaking of which," I said, "have your calls turned up anything solid?"

"Nothing definitive. I'm looking into any similar hit-and-runs. There've been a couple lately, but it's hard to tell if they're related. It would really help if we could nail down the vehicle description."

I shrugged my shoulders sheepishly, ashamed that I couldn't be more precise. "A dark SUV," I said. "That's all I can tell you. I'd say it was black, but I gather one of the others says it might have been navy or some other dark blue. Maybe even dark grey."

"Ya, that's Angie," Sandra said, "the woman from Alliston. At least she came to agree it was an SUV. That helps narrow it down. I'm gonna call her again tomorrow when I go back on shift, see if she's thought about it some more."

I finished the tea in my mug and poured the rest from the pot. Might be time to ask for more hot water. Sandra had already caught George's eye for more coffee. He came by with a pot of each, coffee and hot water. Can't beat good service.

"And speaking of grey," Sandra said, "I have one of the nurses on deck to call me as soon as your friend Gray Bergdorf comes to. He's been in a coma since the accident. I talked with Kang. We're both hoping Bergdorf will be able to give us more info when he wakes up."

"Kang's helping with the other hit-and-runs?"

"Ya. And I've also done a search in our files. We've been comparing notes."

I finished up the last of my breakfast and sat with my tea. Sandra had long since wolfed down hers and was nearly finished her second coffee. I don't imagine she was planning to sleep anytime soon.

Something buzzed. Sandra reached for the cellphone in her pocket, punched in her four-digit password and looked at the message on the screen.

"Damn."

"What's up?"

“It’s my source at the hospital, the nurse.”

“Good news or bad?”

“Sorry, Dugan, it’s bad.”

“How bad?”

“Grayston Bergdorf never woke up from his coma. He died about an hour ago.”

I didn’t know what to say. I just sat there. Finally something came to me.

“Damn. Poor Marcie.”

“Yes,” Sandra said. “And you know what this means…”

I wasn’t sure. But I knew it wasn’t going to be good.

“It means your simple hit-and-run just got more complicated.”

Chapter 26

Arise, and help us
and deliver us for thy mercy's sake.

– Ps. 44, v. 27

Sandra stood up and put on her coat.

"I'd better get back to the newsroom. I should touch base with the dayside desk, let them know in case they want an update story."

I gave her a wan smile and a nod. She was already halfway out the door. It was my turn to pay anyway.

If the desk made her stay to write it, I sure hope they'd count the overtime. Sandra's dedicated and not a clock-watcher. Which is admirable, but also means they sometimes take advantage. A good-natured flexibility, a little informal give and take, was more prevalent in the old days, when the *Gazette* was a small, independent family-owned paper. There was more of a feeling back then of all for one and one for all. But now as one small part of a big faceless – and often heartless – corporation, the union had rightfully become more strict about the terms of the contract. And the staff by necessity more protective of their rights.

No question, I miss the good old days. And having been fired – pardon me, "restructured" – I was glad not to have to be working under the new regime. It was bad enough I had to behave myself for the music committee.

By the time I got home I felt it wasn't too early in the morning to call Marcie. Straight to voicemail on the first ring, so probably she was already talking to someone. Or maybe had turned off her phone, not wanting to talk to anyone. I could understand that. Grief can hit hard, especially that first shock, when you still don't believe it's real. Sometimes you just want to shut out the world and be alone with it.

I know a little something about that.

And then just when you, foolishly, think you might have your emotions under control and you're ready to get back to something resembling a new normal, grief can hit you again. It comes like waves hitting the lakeshore – some of them just small ripples, others bigger breakers that can crash you against the rocks.

Grief sucks, man.

I left Marcie a short message inadequately expressing my sorrow at her loss. And told her to call me if there was anything I could do to help. I had no idea what that might be. But my offer was sincere.

For a second time recently, I began to think about music for the funeral of a friend.

I checked the *Gazette* website. It can't have been even half an hour and Sandra had already filed an update. Only a few hundred words, but still pretty impressive for such a short turnaround:

Hit-and-run
victim dies

Grayston police have renewed calls to the public for any information related to an incident that has resulted in death. Grayston Bergdorf was with friends last Friday, March 14, at Clancy's bar on Grant Street. Bergdorf and a few others were on the sidewalk in front of the bar at approximately 10 p.m. when witnesses say a vehicle struck Bergdorf as he stepped onto the street.

Officer Liu Kang of the Grayston and District Police Department says witness statements suggest the driver of the vehicle did not remain at the scene. He said police are treating it as a hit-and-run accident. Paramedics treated Bergdorf at the scene and rushed him to Grayston General Hospital. A source told the *Gazette* Bergdorf was unconscious when he arrived. He remained in a coma until his death early Monday morning. Pending an investigation, the source said the cause of death was most likely the injuries he sustained in the event.

Bergdorf, 24, who does not live in Grayston, was a singer of classical music with a promising and already accomplished international career. A representative of Bergdorf's talent management was not available for comment at press time.

Kang said witnesses described the suspect vehicle as a dark-colored SUV. He said make and model are not confirmed at this time. Kang said it's possible the vehicle has sustained some damage, likely on the front passenger side.

"We're grateful for the witnesses who have already spoken with us," Kang told the *Gazette*. "We will continue to investigate this incident. We are appealing to anyone who might have further information to speak with us, particularly if they have seen a vehicle matching the description.

"And of course," Kang said, "we implore the driver of the vehicle to seek legal counsel and then come speak to police."

Neat, tight and just under 300 words. Nicely done, Sandra. As always. And "implore." Not a word you see very often in news copy, especially nowadays. Especially coming from a cop. Kang went up a notch or two in my estimation. Maybe I'd even tell him.

I noticed too that Sandra had used what in *Gazette*-speak we call "negative localizing." As a smalltown paper, editors like to play up any local connection they could find. Recent flooding somewhere? Anyone from Grayston injured or dead? Dozens stranded in snowstorm highway pileup? Best check if any Grayston drivers involved. Readers love the local angle.

Of course the opposite is also true. Reporters and deskers would sometimes joke about how far to take it.

"Hey, guys," someone reading the wire might shout out, "there's been a plane crash in Bangladesh."

"How many dead?"

That's always the first question. And the second is like unto it:

"Anybody from Grayston on board?"

"Not sure yet. Story doesn't say."

"OK, that's your deck: 'No Grayston residents confirmed among casualties.'"

Would we actually go that far? Probably not. But that's the standing joke. And the kind of dark humor that helps journalists maintain their sanity in an increasingly chaotic and seemingly insane world. And so in Sandra's story, Gray Bergdorf was "not a Grayston resident." I was glad she hadn't made a Grayston/Grayston pun. Possibly even against resistance from the desk. If so, I'm glad she'd won out against any pressure. You might get away with that kind of flippancy in a puffy feature piece. But not in a serious story reporting his death. I'd expect nothing less from her.

Nothing much beyond the usual happened over the next

few days. Sometimes it's like that. Life just ticks along. At least for those of us still ticking. I again called Marcie and again got her voicemail. I told her not to worry about choir, of course, and to take as much time off as she needed. And again offered to help in any way I could. Even to me that sounded inadequate. But what could I do or say?

I couldn't think of anything. I realized I didn't know much about Gray Bergdorf's personal life. Didn't even know where he lived when he wasn't in Grayston. A bigger city, I assumed. Though nowadays, with an internet connection, you can work from almost anywhere. As a soloist, he probably spent much of his time in hotel or motel rooms, travelling from one gig to another. One of the reasons I was never much keen on a performer's life. For his recordings they probably just rented a church somewhere. Something with good acoustics and minimal traffic noise. Even though the world-renowned Academy of St. Martin in the Fields did indeed give its first concerts in the church after which it named itself (and that still bears the hyphens the chamber orchestra has long since dropped), the band doesn't actually record there. God no. The old Saxon church may have been still "in the fields" when Henry VIII rebuilt it in 1542, but nowadays it's smack in the middle of London at the edge of Trafalgar Square. With all those London cabs and double-decker buses.

Although still highly regarded, you don't hear the Academy quite so often on radio nowadays as in its heyday under its founding conductor. Other groups just as good, some even better, have since popped up. I still remember a favorite *New Yorker* cartoon of a man sitting in an armchair reading a book with a big old stereo system (remember those?) beside him on one side and a parrot on its perch on the other.

The voice from the radio intones: "… played now by the orchestra of St. Martin in the Fields …"

To which the parrot answers, "Neville Marriner conducting."

Such is fame.

Chapter 27

We took sweet counsel together
and walked in the house of God as friends.

– Ps. 55, v. 15

I was again surprised to see Marcie at choir practice, thinking she might not be up to socializing. On the other hand, friends – even casual ones, and I know some of her friendships here run deeper – can be a comfort in times of grief. Something I know firsthand too.

Marcie was quieter than usual. More withdrawn. But still she sang. And seemed to gain some strength from the singing. Music soothes the savage breast, as Congreve says. Maybe it's my bias, but I think choral music can be particularly effective that way. Something about actually breathing together with other people. I'm sure scientists would say it's something to do with our parasympathetic nervous system. Or maybe it just feels good to join a common cause. The word 'conspiracy,' after all, comes from the Latin for 'breathing together.'

I saw her with some of the others at our brief break for juice and cookies – no time for coffee or tea. They were offering their condolences, which Marcie accepted with grace.

With Palm Sunday and Easter fast approaching, that music took up all of our rehearsal time. If we got ahead of it now, I hoped to return to *Messiah* next week. So for now it was *Ride on in Majesty*; *All Glory, Laud and Honor*; *This Joyful Eastertide* and whole bunch of Alleluias of various descriptions. What the heck, we could throw in Handel's *Hallelujah* chorus just to keep in practice.

Which reminded me of our loss of Gray Bergdorf. A personal tragedy, of course. But also on a more selfish, pragmatic level, I wasn't sure what this would do to our looming *Messiah* production. Christine and I had spoken briefly by phone on Monday when I'd called her with the news of his death. But we hadn't decided yet what to do. Should we just cancel the whole thing? That seemed unfair to our singers who had already put in so much work. Should we try to find a replacement alto soloist? Was Cassie McBride really up to the task? Should we press onward but just drop the alto solos? Or keep only a few of the simpler ones? (There goes *Refiner's fire*.)

There was much still to consider. We both thought maybe we should talk to our singers to gauge their feelings. For my part, I was planning to call a little choir meeting after Sunday's service. In the meantime, there was still regular church music to plow through.

Marcie came up to me after rehearsal as everyone was packing up. She was clutching a copy of *Messiah* to her breast. Almost swaddling it, as if it were a baby.

"Hey, Mr. Heywood – Dugan," she said quietly, "have you got a minute?"

"Sure, of course. How are you feeling? I'm so sorry about Gray."

"I'm OK, I guess. And thanks."

She loosened her grip a bit on the music in her hands, looking down on it with affection.

"I found Gray's copy of *Messiah*," she said. "I went looking for it after church last Sunday. I couldn't understand why it had gone missing. It was his personal copy, the one he'd been using since he was a boy. It has all his markings in it."

"I'm glad you found it."

"So am I. It's something I can remember him by."

"Where was it?"

"That's the thing," she said. "I found it stuffed in among the spare copies in that bottom cubbyhole. I don't know how it got there. Gray wouldn't have put it there."

"Maybe he put it down somewhere and forgot," I said. "Someone else picked it up and just put it on the pile."

"I guess," Marcie said. "Still doesn't make sense."

"Well at least you found it," I said, trying to sound helpful.

"Yes," she said. "But here's the crazy thing: Someone's defaced it. There's scribbling all over it."

Chapter 28

Forget not the voice of thine enemies:
the tumult of them that hate thee
increaseth ever more and more.

– Ps. 74, v. 23

Marcie opened the music to the title page. Someone had taken a heavy black pen or marker and scrawled all over it. You could hardly read the text underneath all the random black lines.

"At first I thought it might have been some little kid from the Sunday School or the toddlers' day care," she said. "It does kinda look like some child went crazy with a crayon."

"It does." But I sensed there was more coming.

"But then I looked more carefully," she said. "Take a look. It doesn't seem random at all."

By this time, all the other singers had put away their music and chairs, put on their coats and left. I'd barely noticed them leaving. Marcie and I were alone, the score in front of us on the lid of the old piano.

I slowly turned the pages. Nothing seemed amiss for the first few, the opening orchestral *Sinfonia*. The first clue came a few pages on, in the opening tenor solo. In the phrase "speak ye comfortably to Jerusalem, and cry unto her that her warfare is accomplish'd, that her iniquity is pardoned," someone had drawn heavy underlines on the words 'warfare' and 'iniquity.' But not, I noticed, on 'pardoned.'

This did not seem like the random scribbling of some toddler with a crayon. It was more purposeful than that.

I skipped ahead. The next few pages – the *Glory to God*

first chorus and the bass recit *Thus Saith the Lord* – seemed untouched, other than a few breath markings in the alto part of the chorus, just where you might expect a singer to put them.

And then I got to the first big alto solo, *But who may abide/ Refiner's fire* – the one Gray had done such an impressive job with at our rehearsals.

The entire first page was covered with more heavy black scrawls and scribbles. But now it was looking less like a careless toddler and more like an angry tantrum. The other pages of the aria had a single line through them, as if someone were just dismissing them out of hand.

This was not random. This was calculated. There was method in this madness.

A further look through the rest of the score confirmed my suspicions. In the recit and aria *For behold, darkness shall cover the Earth/The people that walked in darkness* – a bass solo section Gray would have no reason to notate – someone had underlined every instance of the word 'darkness' (also 'gross darkness'). The alto solo near the beginning of Part II also had scratches across the opening page and heavy underlining of the words 'despisèd,' 'rejected,' also 'sorrows' and 'grief.' And in later solos and choruses, heavy lines under – sometimes a box around – every instance of the words 'dead' and 'death.' Of which there are many. A lot of talk of death. No question, the *Messiah* texts are morbid, if ultimately redemptive.

Marcie stood silent as I went through the pages, waiting for me to confirm what she'd obviously already concluded.

Someone really hated Grayston Bergdorf.

Chapter 29

From my youth up I am in misery and ready to die;
thy terrors have I suffered with a troubled mind.

– Ps. 88, v. 16

"Wow," I said. "Do you have any idea who would have done this?

"I can't be sure," Marcie said. "But I think I know."

And so she told me: She and Gray had been dating for a little over a year, she said. They'd started getting serious only in the past few months.

Part of that, Marcie said, was because Gray was still getting over, still recovering from, a previous relationship that had, as Marcie put it, "ended badly."

"Kinda spectacularly badly, to be honest," she said. "Gray didn't like to talk about it. Didn't really go into much detail. But from what I gather it was pretty messy."

Well, I thought, relationships break up all the time. Doesn't have to be a big deal. Sometimes it takes a while to realize maybe you just aren't compatible. That despite your best efforts, it's just not working. Or the spark isn't there. Hell, Priya and I were together for more than a year and I know we really cared for each other. But even we had to admit it probably wasn't going to work out long term. But we were lucky – our friendship survived the breakup.

Other couples aren't so lucky. Maybe one of them cheats on the other. I didn't really see either Gray or Marcie as the cheating type, but you never know. Maybe Gray's ex cheated on him and he broke it off.

"So what happened?" I said. "Do you know?"

"Like I said, he didn't talk about it much," Marcie said. "But he was definitely the one who broke it off."

"Did she cheat on him?"

"Oh no, nothing like that. It had more to do with her personal issues. She had a lot of problems."

"What kind of problems?"

"He said she was very possessive," Marcie said. "Carla was jealous for no reason. Always checking up on him, on his every move. Always hounding him with questions, making him account for every minute he was away from her."

"Did she have any reason to be so suspicious?"

"God no! You've met Gray. He's a sweetheart. *Was* a sweetheart," she said with a catch in her throat.

I let a beat go by so Marcie could catch her breath.

"Is that all?"

"No," Marcie said. "There was a lot more going on. Carla had major anxiety attacks over everything. I feel badly – and I'm sure Gray did – because she obviously had some mental health issues. No formal diagnosis and she wasn't taking any prescribed meds. Started drinking and taking drugs to calm down. First just a little weed to relax. But then she started drinking more and more. And then she started on street drugs. Booze, painkillers, drugs – whatever she could get her hands on. That pretty quickly got out of control and made everything worse.

"I think there were some big fights before Gray finally ended it," Marcie said. "Nothing physical, nothing like that. At least not from him. But some shouting, for sure. She'd get mad and throw dishes."

"So what made him end it?"

"An accumulation of things, I guess," Marcie said. "Her

drug use ramped up. She was able to hide it for a while, but it started to catch up with her. She didn't have a job. Gray was lending her money he thought was for groceries or job interviews or her phone bill. But it turned out she was using."

"And by 'using' you mean doing drugs."

"Ya, that's the terminology. So all that money was just going for booze. Or up in smoke. Or up her nose. Gray helped get her into rehab once. Things got better briefly but that didn't last."

"Rehab only works if the user is serious about quitting."

"Exactly. Pretty soon, she was back to the lying and the stealing and all the excuses. Addicts will lie about anything to get what they want."

"Must have been tough for Gray."

"It was," Marcie said. "Like I said, he didn't really talk much about it. What I've told you comes from me piecing together little bits of conversation we've had.

"Anyway, he finally had to cut her off. Get Carla out of his life. For his own sake. And hers."

"And I gather she didn't take that well."

"No, not at all," Marcie said. "Gray said he even thought about getting a restraining order. In the end he didn't."

"So what happened? Where is she now?"

"I'm not sure. In one of her more lucid moments, Gray did manage to help her pack up her things and move out. I think last time he saw her, she was couch surfing with some old friend of hers."

"But not in rehab."

"No. And it wasn't til after she was gone that he found some of the sabotage."

"Sabotage?"

"Yes. She'd scratched big gouges in some of his favorite LPs. Taken CDs out of the case and tossed them in the trash. Smashed his favorite mug. Ripped up some of his shirts. Just silly, destructive things to get back at him."

"I'm sensing a pattern," I said. "So, do you think she's the one who marked up Gray's copy of *Messiah*?"

"I do," Marcie said. "It's certainly the kind of thing she would do in a fit of anger to spite him."

"The question," I said, "assuming she's the one who did it, is when?"

"I've been thinking about that myself," Marcie said. "It's possible she did it ages ago, way back when they broke up."

"But wouldn't Gray have noticed that?"

"Maybe – although it's been more than a year since he performed it. So he might not have even looked at his score until now, for this gig."

"Wouldn't he have told you – like when he came here the first time for rehearsal?"

"Maybe. Or maybe not. Maybe he saw it but didn't want to upset me. But that's not what worries me."

"What's that?" I asked, though I'm pretty sure I knew what she meant.

"What worries me," Marcia said, "is that Carla has come back to haunt us. One time when Gray and I were out for a walk, he seemed nervous – which was not like him. He seemed distracted. Kept looking over his shoulder. When I asked him what was wrong, he finally told me. He thought maybe he'd seen Carla following us."

"Here in Grayston?" I said.

"Yes. And said he thought he'd seen her at least once before. But when he turned to look, she was gone. He was worried maybe she'd followed him here. Like, stalking him."

"Did you ever see her?"

"No," Marcie said. "I never did. And Gray later said he must have just imagined it."

"But you're not sure."

"I don't know what to think," Marcie said. "But I'm worried that maybe she *is* here. And that somehow she found a way to sneak into the choir room without anyone noticing and trash Gray's score now as a new way to get back at him."

"Well," I said, "there were a lot of extra people milling around the church hall that night we had the first joint choir rehearsal. Maybe Carla was able to sneak in then in all the confusion."

"I suppose that's possible."

"But do you think she's still so angry at him that she'd come to down to stalk him. And take her anger out on his music score?"

"Worse than that," Marcie said. "I think Carla may have been the one who ran him down in that damn SUV that killed him."

Chapter 30

He cast upon them the fury of his wrath, anger,
displeasure and trouble:
a band of destroying angels.

– Ps. 78, v. 51

I took a moment for the implications of that to sink in.

"Marcie, do you really think Gray's ex deliberately ran him over and then drove away without stopping?"

"Do you mean do I think she meant to kill him?" Marcie said. "I don't know. I'm not sure of anything, really. Maybe she was just trying to scare him. Maybe she just wasn't thinking straight. But if she were drunk, or high – or both – maybe she wasn't fully in control of her driving. And I'm assuming she would have been angry. In a rage."

"But you have no real evidence," I said. "You didn't see her behind the wheel."

"I barely had time to register anything. And with the rain, it was hard to see. Just a big, dark blob. I stooped down to look at Gray. I really only saw it when I looked up and it was driving away. It was only when I was talking to that police officer afterwards that I realized it was probably an SUV, just because it seemed bigger than a normal car."

"Yes, they are that," I said. "Have you told the police your suspicions about Carla?"

"I have," she said. "After finding his *Messiah* score on Sunday morning, I phoned that Officer Kang that afternoon and spoke with him about it."

"What did he say?"

"Oh, he said he'd make a note of it in his file," she said.

"But I don't think he seemed to think it was very important."

"Well, I don't mean to be dismissive, but absent any evidence it would likely be hard to prove."

"Ya, that's kinda what he said."

Marcie took Gray's copy of *Messiah* and again cradled it in her arms.

"I just can't believe he's gone." Her voice was small.

I didn't know what else to say. Sometimes it's best not to say anything.

Marcie looked up at me. With a little more strength in her voice, she spoke:

"Even now that Gray's … dead," her voice caught on that word, "it seems like the police are just going to dismiss this as a random accident."

"Which it could well be," I said. I hate playing devil's advocate. But sometimes you have to.

"I know that's a possibility," she said. "Maybe it's even likely. But if there's even a chance that Carla did this to him – by accident or on purpose – I want to know. Gray deserves that."

She looked up at me again. I thought of that word 'implore.'

"He doesn't have any family, you know," she said. "He's an only child and both his parents are dead. He has an uncle in England somewhere I think, but they were never close. I'm the closest thing he has to family. Will you help me?"

"What would you like me to do?" I said – though I had a pretty good idea where this was headed. My reputation preceded me.

"Would you talk to the police?" she said. "I know you've

worked with them before. Maybe they'll pay more attention to you than to me."

"You know I'm not *with* the police, right?" I said. "And I'm not even a reporter anymore. I don't have the paper backing me."

"You didn't the last two times either," Marcie said matter-of-factly. She seemed to be gaining confidence since she'd put her case to me. "And yet you helped the police solve two murders. One they didn't even think was a murder in the first place. You convinced them."

I almost said something flippant about Marcie becoming my PR agent, but thought better of it. Not the right time to be glib.

"OK," I said. "I'll talk to Kang and see what he says. But no promises. I'm not exactly his favorite person. And it's not like a have any pull."

"More than I have," she said reasonably.

"I do have one other friend on the force," I said, thinking of Don Patterson. "I can loop him in, if Kang hasn't already. But again – no promises."

"Thanks, Mr. Hey– Dugan," she said, smiling. It was like I'd taken a load off her shoulders.

When in doubt, call for reinforcements. After Marcie left, I locked up and went home. Took Wolf out for her final pee. And sent a text to Sandra Novak. I figured she'd be starting her lobster shift soon.

"Breakfast Friday?" I texted. *"My treat."*

A few moments later my phone chimed. *Dun-dun.*

"2x in 1 wk?" her text said. *"sure. cu then."*

So, Maggie's at 7 it was.

Chapter 31

It is but lost labour that ye haste to rise up early, and so late take rest and eat the bread of carefulness; for so he giveth his beloved sleep.
– Ps. 127, v. 3

“So you’re telling me this girl thinks her boyfriend’s ex ran him over with her car? Er, SUV?”

Sandra, a woman in her 30s, could get away with calling Marcie, a woman in her 20s, a ‘girl.’ Certainly not something I’d dare to say.

“That’s what she told me,” I said. “And from the looks of things, she’s got some good reasons to think so.”

“But no actual evidence.”

“Beyond a scribbled music score? And from what Gray has told her of their, um, difficult relationship? Beyond that no real evidence. Just a hunch.”

“I respect hunches,” Sandra said. “I can work with hunches.”

Spoken like a true journalist.

Maggie’s seemed busier this morning than it had been when we were here Monday. In fact, most Mondays. There seemed to be a few more students in the joint, fueling up for a weekend of partying. And a few more office and retail workers. I spotted at least two city councillors and a couple of lawyers. With the back of city hall right across the street, it wouldn’t surprise me if the mayor showed up.

Our server was a student too. One of the endless rotation of students working part-time as they work their way through school. She was pleasant but looked sleepy. Probably not used to being up so early in the morning. Or maybe had pulled an all-nighter to finish a paper. I don't miss that part of my student days.

George himself was at his usual spot at cash up front, greeting coming and departing patrons, with his usual "Good morning, Senator" as they arrived or "Thank you, Senator" as they paid their bill and left.

The diner wasn't as crazy busy as I knew it would be on Saturday. But it was getting there. Good for George.

Sandra and I had finished our breakfasts and were lingering over our second mugs of coffee and tea, respectively. I'd filled her in on my conversation with Marcie from the night before and her suspicions about Gray's ex Carla.

"What's her name again?"

"Lumeti," I said. "Carla Lumeti. I don't know her age, but I'd guess around the same as Gray's – 24 or 5."

Sandra made a note in her reporter's steno pad. It was like a regular ring-bound steno pad but half the width. And it had the *Gazette's* nameplate on the front cover. In my days as a reporter, I'd probably filled hundreds of them. Good thing they were a perk that came with the job. I wondered if Blackwell was still supplying them or if this was left over from the previous owner's generosity.

"That name hasn't come up in any of my research," Sandra said. "But then, I wasn't looking for it. I'll take another look in the files."

By which I knew she meant the electronic database, not the musty old room in the basement filled with actual filing cabinets. Funny how technology advances but we still cling to old terminology. Do people still talk of 'dialing' a phone number?

"I've found three other hit-and-runs in the past 20 months

or so," Sandra said. "But no actual SUVs. Two of them were definitely small or compact cars. One was a pickup truck. And the driver of that one had too much to drink and drove it into a telephone pole all by himself. Wasn't going very fast, thankfully, so damage mostly to the truck and telephone pole, less to him. But it takes him out of the running as a possible suspect."

"Unless he got himself an SUV."

"Possible, I suppose," Sandra said. "But he'd be driving on a suspended licence. With at least another three months to go. Probably wouldn't risk it."

"I wouldn't be so sure," I said. "Anyone stupid enough to drive drunk might also be stupid enough to drive without a licence."

"Fair point."

Sandra took a final swallow of her coffee and looked down at the empty mug. I could tell she was weighing whether to ask for a refill. Or whether two was her limit at this moment.

"Have you talked to Kang about this?" she said. "Or your pal Don Patterson?"

"Not yet. Marcie just told me last night. I was thinking of sloping over there today to see if either of them is on duty."

"Pretty sure Kang is," she said. "We're supposed to touch base later this morning."

"Haven't you finished your shift? Shouldn't you go home and sleep?"

"Ya, well, we're short-handed," she said with a shrug. "As always. It's just a phone call to see if he has any updates. I can do that from home. I'd fob it off on another reporter if we had lots. But we don't. And besides, this is still my story."

"Well, don't let the union rep know you're doing freebies – unless you're claiming overtime."

"OT? It is to laugh. But ya, I'll tiptoe carefully around the union rep. I don't want to get on her bad side."

The *Gazette's* union rep is a bit of a legend. Tough as nails, which is who you want on your side when the contract is up. Rumor has it she'd served time – though whether for boosting a car or Murder 1 no one knows. Her juvey record is sealed and she's not talking. She likes to keep people guessing, especially when talking to management. It makes her seem even tougher at the bargaining table. Which has always worked out well for the rank and file. And there was no point asking my friend Patrick – I was still struggling not to call him Carrot Top – about her. She's closer to my age, so they wouldn't have done their juvey time together. Patrick would still have been in diapers. If he was even born yet. Don't ask me to do math in my head.

"Have you talked to Patterson lately?"

"Not for a few months," I said. "His boy dropped out of my choir. Didn't come back in the fall. He said choir was taking time away from his basketball and soccer. So we haven't had any contact."

"Ah, adolescence," Sandra said. "Probably wants to start dating too."

"Could be," I said. "Or soon, anyway. Also his voice was breaking. Always an awkward transition for a boy. I'm hoping he may come back next year when he's settled down. I'd hate to waste that musical training. And he's a nice kid."

"Well, if you haven't talked with Patterson in a while, he'll have a little surprise for you."

"Oh yeah? What's that?"

Sandra smiled.

"I'll let him fill you in."

Chapter 32

Man goeth forth to his work
and to his labour until the evening.

– Ps. 104, v. 24

Sandra left and I went to the front, paying the bill and my regards to George. After all, I'd said it was my treat.

Soon I was back at the police station, where I'd been less than a week before. What with everything that's happened in the past couple of years, it seems I've found myself at the cop shop more often as a civilian that I ever had as a newspaper reporter. Not even when I was doing stints on the cop beat, since most of that was just checking in by phone anyway.

Standing at the sergeant's desk looking over across the bullpen – which reminded me so much of a newsroom, with clacking keyboards and phones ringing – I saw Kang in one of the little windowed side offices. He was talking on the phone. Maybe even to Sandra. He looked up, saw me and waved a 'hang on a minute' gesture. I told the sergeant I'd wait.

In a few moments, Kang came over and stuck out his hand to shake mine.

"Mr. Heywood, good morning," he said. "I'd ask what brings you here, but I probably know already."

"Just checking in to see if you've made any progress on the Grayston Bergdorf case."

"See? I knew that," Kang said with at least half a smile. "I must be psychic."

I could tell Kang had still not fully warmed to me. But I

found that half-smile encouraging. Maybe he was learning to tolerate me. We'd crossed paths twice now, both times when I found myself helping the police solve a murder. In the case of Priya, they hadn't even thought it was murder at first. Just an accident. After my conversation with Marcie, I was afraid I might have to fight that battle again.

Kang led me back across the bullpen, weaving between desks and back to the little office where I'd first seen him.

"Have a seat," he said, shutting the door most of the way to tamp down the noise but not closing it completely. Good. Made me feel less like I was a suspect. Or a truant schoolboy sent to the principal's office.

Kang perched on the corner of the desk.

"I was just on the phone to Novak," he said. "And since I know you guys are pals and she'll probably tell you what I told her anyway, I might as well save her the step."

I nodded and smiled. Mr. Friendly.

"I'm afraid we still don't have much to go on," Kang said. "As far as we're concerned, it's still a hit-and-run accident. Thanks to eyewitnesses, including yourself, we're looking for a dark SUV. Possibly black, but dark anyway. Make and model unknown. Quite possibly with some body damage on the front passenger side. We've put out a BOLO and we've checked the local garages and bodyshops. But if some hobbyist is going to fix it on his own, there's not much we can do about that. And even an idiot could probably figure out how to fix a crumpled fender by checking videos on YouTube. We've looked into some other recent hit-and-runs, but nothing much came of that."

"Now that Gray is dead, how does that change things?"

"Well, obviously it makes a difference when we come

to charging someone," Kang said. "There's a big difference between 'failure to remain' and 'negligent homicide.' Or whatever the charges will be. But that comes later. My first priority is to find and catch whoever did this. That part doesn't really change."

"But surely a dead victim is more important to solve than an injured one."

"That's true," he said. "It certainly makes it more urgent. Especially because we don't want this idiot to get behind the wheel drunk again and hit someone else."

"So you're assuming it was a drunk driver?"

"Ah, Mr. Heywood, you should know that police don't like working from assumptions. Just like reporters don't. But yes, until any other evidence surfaces, I'd say that's the most likely scenario."

I knew Marcie had spoken with Kang about her suspicions about Carla, the ex-girlfriend. I wondered if I should mention it. Kang beat me to it.

"And before you ask – yes, Ms. Harding has spoken with me about this ex-girlfriend –" Kang looked down a some papers on the desk "– Ms. Lumeti. And her suspicions in that regard."

"And?"

"And," Kang said. "We will look into it. And give it any proper attention it deserves."

That didn't sound very encouraging. More like a dismissal. But I also knew better than to press my luck with Kang any further.

And sure enough, Kang stood up. He was dismissing me, probably as much as he was dismissing the theory of the troubled ex-girlfriend.

"That's all, Mr. Heywood," Kang said, opening the door, gesturing me out and walking me briskly across the room. "Thanks for coming in."

I'm not sure how sincerely he meant that.

"I shouldn't have to remind you but I will anyway," he said as we reached the front desk, "please leave the policing to the police. We're professionals. And we *do* know what we're doing. I promise you we'll keep looking into this accident."

"Thank you," I said. "I appreciate that."

And I do appreciate it. But much as I generally respect the police – at least Kang and the other ones I know – I also know that, like the few remaining reporters and deskers in the newsroom, they were fighting an uphill battle against an increasing workload and diminishing resources. I don't doubt Kang's ability, nor his commitment. But I do doubt how much of those he'd be able to continue devoting to what in his mind is just a simple accident.

So whether he liked it or not, I was going to continue to stick my nose in where he thinks it doesn't belong. I owe that to Marcie. And to Gray. And also in some ways to my wife and daughter. We need to keep drunk drivers off the roads.

In the meantime, since I was already here, I might as well check in on my old friend Officer Don Patterson.

Chapter 33

The Lord rewarded me after my righteous dealing;
according to the cleanness of my hands did he recompense me.
– Ps. 18, v. 22

With Kang safely out of sight, I turned again to the desk sergeant.

"Is Officer Don Patterson on duty?" I said. I looked around the bullpen and didn't see him. "I'd like to speak with him if he has a moment. Thanks."

The duty sergeant looked at me. It seemed to be my day for getting half-smiles.

"I'm sorry," he said. "We have no Officer Don Patterson on staff."

Really? That was news to me. I gave him my best befuddled look. Which was easy, since befuddled was definitely what I was feeling.

"However," he said, his smile widening just a bit, "*Lieutenant* Don Patterson might be available. I'll check and see if he's in."

He was. So the sergeant directed me down the hall to my right.

"Second door on your left," he said.

The door was partly ajar, with a plaque that said, "Lt. Don Patterson, Homicide." I knocked lightly.

"Enter!"

So I did. Don Patterson – *Lt.* Don Patterson – rose from behind his desk – with an impressive window behind that – and gave me a full smile. No half-measures here.

"Dugan!" he said, his smile turning into a grin. "Good to see you."

He came around the desk and shook my hand. Which seemed awfully formal for someone I've considered a friend for more than a decade, since he was a beat cop doing PR and I was a reporter covering the cop beat.

A flack and a hack, that was us.

"Jeez, Don," I said. "I look the other way for a few months and they're handing out promotions to just anybody!"

"C'mon, Dugan," he said. "Give me credit. I bought this one fair and square."

Why do men tease and joke with each other as a lame form of affection? We're still not always good at showing our emotions. But I gave it a try.

"Seriously, though," I said. "Congratulations! I know you've worked hard for it. When did this happen?"

"Thanks. Couple of months ago. Your old pal-slash-nemesis Silipo took early retirement. So there was an opening for lieutenant."

Ah, that magic formula where cops and some other public servents get to retire early after a certain length of service. Journalists, being private sector, ain't so lucky. And church music directors? Forget it.

Like Kang, Lt. Andy Silipo and I had crossed paths over those past two murder investigations I'd found myself wrapped up in. More like crossed swords, really. Kang was second fiddle, but Silipo had been the investigation officer on both cases. And had made it pretty clear he didn't like an amateur like me pissing in his pond. Although, to be fair, once I'd actually been of some help he'd grudgingly acknowledged some gratitude.

I wondered, now that Don was in his shoes, whether that would make my reluctant task easier or harder. Would Don be like Silipo and close ranks to keep me away? I guess I'd find out.

"So, let me guess," Patterson said, taking his seat behind the desk and gesturing me to one of the two chairs facing him. He looked serious. Uh-oh. This time it felt more like a job interview.

"Now that the accident involving your friend Grayston Bergdorf has resulted in his death," Patterson said, "and now that his girlfriend has a theory that it might not have been an accident but instead the act of a crazy ex-girlfriend, she's asked you to investigate, since she doesn't trust us to do the job properly and because you have somehow earned yourself a reputation as some sort of fancy Sherlock. Have I got that about right?"

"Well …"

"And you do know," he continued sternly, "that it is the official policy of this department – hell, of *any* police department – that civilians, amateurs, have no place in the investigative process. And that in fact we consider them more often a hindrance that in some cases can border on obstruction of justice. Which I'm sure you'll agree can have very serious consequences. Do we understand each other?"

I didn't know what to say. I probably looked a bit cowed. Which I'm sure was Don's intention.

The air hung heavy and silent between us for a moment. Don broke the silence with another grin.

"Ha!" he said. "How did you like my little speech? I've been practising it."

I felt my muscles unclench. I hadn't even realized how tense he'd made me.

"Nice," I said. "You got me."

"Well, I'm half-serious," Patterson said. "I'm giving you the official department policy. And I do mean it. But with a minor caveat. If it were anyone else, they'd get the full speech and a swift kick out the door.

"But because it's you and because you *have* actually helped us in the past, you get a bit of a pass. Or at least some leeway that I wouldn't give to just anybody else. But the basics remain. Don't get in our way. And don't piss off Kang. He's a good cop and he doesn't need any more grief than he's already got."

"Thanks," I said. "I'll be careful."

Don nodded.

"OK, now that we've got that out of the way, have you actually got anything useful to tell us?"

"It sounds like you and Kang both are pretty much up to speed," I said. "Or way ahead of me. I gather he's told you about Marcie's suspicions regarding the troubled ex-girlfriend?"

"Lumeti? Yes, he has. And troubled. I should have said troubled, not crazy. Sorry about that. Certainly have to be careful not to say that word in public."

"Did Marcie show you the scribbled-up copy of the music?"

"No, and not to Kang either. But she did describe it."

"Well, I *have* seen it," I said. "And I can tell you it's legit scary. This is not just some random scribbling. This is someone who's really pissed – maybe even borderline psychotic – acting out some pretty destructive anger issues.

It's disturbing. Especially considering what happened afterward."

"Assuming it *was* the ex-girlfriend," Patterson said. "And assuming the two events – the mutilated book and the hit-and-run – are even related."

"Yes, I supposed they could be unrelated," I said. "But that doesn't get us very far."

"True," Patterson said. "What's that expression doctors use? 'When you hear hooves, think horses, not zebras.'"

"That's the one. So, have you been able to track down Carla Lumeti?"

"We have not," he said. "She has no police record. Not for drunk driving. Not even for speeding. Couple of parking tickets, but nothing recent. And the address on her driver's licence seems to be out of date. We've made some calls but we haven't tracked her down."

"That may be hard," I said. "She's an addict and may have fallen off the wagon. May be using again. Marcie says the last she knew, Carla was couch surfing somewhere. Anywhere. If that's the case, she may be hard to find."

"Right," Patterson said. "And I'm sure Kang or Novak has told you the other hit-and-runs we've found so far haven't led us anywhere useful. We've also had a few complaints of what seems to be some kids bombing around that neighborhood at night, making noise and squealing tires. There was even one from the night your friend was hit."

"Was it an SUV?"

"Could be. These are usually neighbors calling in to the complaint line. They don't provide a lot of detail. Most of them don't even leave their names. Kinda hard for us to follow up. But we'll keep an eye out."

"So where does that leave us?"

"Well," he said, spreading his arms to encompass his office and by extension the entire police department, "it leaves *us* continuing our investigation as best we can. We'll try to find this Carla Lumeti and question her. We'll continue checking garages and bodyshops and dealerships for a damaged SUV. And we'll hope maybe some other witness will come forward. Someone who may have seen the vehicle flee the scene. With any luck can ID the driver."

Patterson put his arms down, looked at me and shrugged. "I'm not sure where that leaves *you*."

Chapter 34

So that the sun shall not burn thee by day,
neither the moon by night.

– Ps. 121, v. 6

Breakfast with Sandra had postponed my usual early morning kayak. I was overdue. Just as well: I needed to think and the pleasant monotony of paddling sometimes helps give order to my thoughts. Once I got home and changed into my gear – most of the ice was gone but the water was still frigid, so the wetsuit remained prudent – I walked the 'yak down to the shore, put in and soon was on my way.

It was good to be back out on the water. Cold, but relatively calm. And despite a lot of cloud cover, the sun broke through for an occasional appearance. There wasn't enough wind for any sailboats or sailboarders. And I didn't see nor hear any sign of Carrot Top – Patrick – or any other speedboats. This time of year I still have the lake mostly to myself.

I paddled away from shore. East toward downtown or west toward the hospital and campus? Since the sun was far from blinding – no paddling to Damascus for me – I set off for downtown. Might as well enjoy any brightness that might come my way. So little of it this time of year.

Dip. Pull. Wrist.

Dip. Pull. Wrist.

Intellectually, I wasn't feeling very bright at all. Mostly confused. Overwhelmed by too much information, none of it seemingly very useful. Not sure how much help I would be to Marcie. Or the police, for that matter. Not that they necessarily needed my help.

What did we know? We had Grayston Bergdorf, a talented and likable guy, run down in the street by a driver unknown in a vehicle unknown and for reasons unknown. Barring any further information, the police were treating it as unintentional. A random act, most likely by a drunk driver. Or possibly a very inexperienced driver. Either way, someone not fully in control of the vehicle. Or maybe just not fully in control of their emotions.

So, drunk driving or road rage? And if road rage, was it generalized or focused specifically on Gray? In other words, was this accidental or deliberate? And either way, who was driving?

I paddled some more as I passed the yacht club, its patio furniture still locked up and covered for the winter. It would be another month at least, probably two, before it might be warm enough to entice diners to the outdoors. And then only if the weather were nice.

Dip. Pull. Wrist.

Dip. Pull. Wrist.

OK. If it were just some random drunk or inept driver, that doesn't help me much. Or more important, Marcie. And anyway, Don and Kang and any other cops were better equipped to handle that line of investigation. They could check vehicle registries and licence plates with resources not available to me. Especially if we got lucky and some other witness came forward with a better description of the vehicle and/or driver. Maybe even a partial plate. But no luck so far.

Sandra had already helped by searching out similar hit-

and-runs, but that hadn't yielded anything useful either. At least not so far.

So what could *I* do? Right. Let's assume, for the sake of argument, it *wasn't* random. *Wasn't* an accident. But someone had deliberately aimed their vehicle – again, for the sake argument, let's agree it's an SUV – at Gray Bergdorf specifically. Then the question is who? And the other question is why? And in fact there's a third question: Did the driver really intend to kill Gray or just injure him? Or even just scare him?

Which brings us back to whether the driver was drunk – not thinking clearly and not fully in control of the SUV – or merely inept.

Dip. Pull. Wrist.

Dip. Pull. Wrist.

I'd reached the downtown core. To my left rose city hall in all its stolid splendor, its greened copper dome dully reflecting whatever light it could from the sun that was now a bit higher in the sky. And beyond that the greened copper spire of St. Nicholas church, once the holder of many secrets, most of which I hope are now revealed. I don't know if the town could survive much more of that unfolding scandal. There was still much healing to be done.

If not merely accidental, I suspect that made it less likely the driver was drunk. Or at least blindingly drunk. That'd be more likely if it were random. Maybe a little liquid courage to steel oneself to the job, but not so drunk that he – or she – didn't fully intend to do it.

But again, do what? Run over Gray to kill him? That would take a pretty high level of rage. Murder is a big step from anger. Or hit him just enough to inflict a little damage? Make him suffer some of the pain the driver himself – or herself – was feeling? (English really does need a useable set of gender-neutral pronouns. Themself I guess will have to serve in the meantime.)

If that's the case, the addict ex-girlfriend Carla Lumeti most closely fits the bill. Assuming Marcie is right in thinking it was Carla who took a black marker to Gray's *Messiah* score, Carla seems a likely suspect for someone acting out her anger at Gray in the most destructive way. But that still leaves the question of how far Carla was willing to take her anger.

Dip. Pull. Wrist.

Dip. Pull. Wrist.

But hang on a minute. Carla's not the only one – that we already know of – who might be mad at Gray. And who knows? There may be more. Cassie McBride, for one, might feel she lost out on her chance for a big alto solo debut because this hotshot countertenor waltzed in at the last minute and stole her spotlight. But would that make a young girl jealous enough to run him over? I know adolescence can be a time of emotional turmoil. But this? Seems unlikely. Besides, did Cassie even know how to drive? That's something I'd have to check. Maybe she only meant to play chicken with Gray, scare him a little bit but, as an inexperienced driver, lost control of that big SUV. Maybe it was a bigger vehicle than she's used to driving. But then how would she have access to it?

Too many questions.

Chapter 35

Righteousness and justice
are the foundation of thy throne.

– Ps. 89, v. 14

I'd paddled my way past city hall and the main drag and nearly arrived at the causeway and lift bridge that separate Grayston from the township next door to the south. I made a quick backpaddle/frontpaddle turn – it's good to keep in practice – and headed back home.

Dip. Pull. Wrist.

Dip. Pull. Wrist.

For the sake of completeness, if nothing else, there are a few more people I should include in my inventory. Cassie wasn't the only one with eyes on the solo prize. Margaret McBride was a leading contender in the race for pushiest stage mother. Or as we'd call her today, a helicopter parent – though Mrs. McBride seemed more like a bulldozer parent than a helicopter one.

My magpie brain did that word nerd thing where it darted off on a tangent. Funny word, 'helicopter.' You might think – if you were nerdy and thought of such things at all – it would be a combination of earlier words, maybe Latin or Greek, like 'heli' and 'copter.' Helix, like a spiral or coil or spring or DNA, would give us 'heli.' Which would leave us with 'copter.' Whatever that is.

But in fact it's not. Or not quite. It's actually helico-pter. 'Helico' like helix and 'pter' from the Greek word for wing – like that flying dinosaur the pterodactyl.

Huh. And here ended the first lesson.

But in fact my little tangent had taken me somewhere useful, as they sometimes do. Maybe my brain is smarter than I am. It took me to DNA. And to realizing that, unlike the last time I found myself involved with a murder in Grayston, DNA – even assuming we could find any – would likely not help us ID the killer this time. At least last time it gave the police a list of possible suspects. Even if our drunk driver already had a criminal record, I don't think they'd left any DNA at the scene. Unless maybe they tossed out a cigarette butt. Or a beer can. I don't remember hearing a beer can. But I couldn't swear to it.

And yes – accident or not – whoever was driving that SUV is now officially a killer. It would be up to the courts to determine what kind, whether accidental death or negligent homicide or manslaughter or outright murder. Or whatever else the police might have in mind. Not my job to decide, thankfully. Only my job, if I could, to help find and identify the driver. And let the justice system take it from there. There was only a rough kind of justice for my family. The drunk driver who'd killed them had immediately smashed himself into a rock face.

But back to my suspect list: Margaret McBride certainly has ambitions for her daughter's success. Quite possibly, from what I've seen, even stronger ambitions than the daughter herself. Would that ambition – vicarious ambition at that – send her into a frenzy enough to propel about 5,000 pounds of rubber and steel at her daughter's perceived rival? After defacing his copy of *Messiah*? Assuming she did either of those things. Maybe they're not even related. Maybe Carla trashed the music and Mrs. McBride drove the SUV. Or vice versa.

Or maybe I'm just imagining connections where none exist. Putting together unconnected pieces as if they were part of a larger puzzle. That's what Sherlock does. And all those other detectives in the mystery novels I like to read. The books that take up a good chunk of linear footage on my bookshelves.

But life's rarely like that. Most often, the pieces don't fit. Mostly stuff just happens and there's no rhyme nor reason to it. I certainly don't believe there's some grand divine design. If there is, the designer seems pretty careless at times. Or inept. Or even cruel. Just ask my dead wife and child.

Oh, that's right: You can't.

Dip. Pull. Wrist.

Dip. Pull. Wrist.

Cassie's father, Harold McBride. Now *there's* a possibility. From what her choir director Christine Tanaka has told me, he sounds overprotective of his daughter. Castrating pigs indeed. Imagine what else he might do if he thought his daughter were at risk.

Fathers can be dangerous. The summer I was 15, I briefly had a girlfriend, also 15, a lovely girl named Jacqueline. Her mother liked me but her father, strictly Roman Catholic, didn't want his daughter to have anything to with boys. And if he'd found out I wasn't Catholic – not even Christian – hoo boy! So we had to do a certain amount of sneaking around behind his back. We'd meet up in the evening when Jackie was walking the family dog and just stroll around her neighborhood and talk. We'd hold hands. There was a bit of kissing. But that's all. Scout's honor. It was all very innocent. We were only 15, after all.

One fine summer's evening, at the end of our walk, we were sitting quietly on the back step, holding hands and whispering so her father wouldn't hear us. After a few moments, we heard the *thump-thump-thump* of her father clomping down the basement stairs.

"That's my dad," Jackie whispered. "You'd better go."

But of course I didn't want to.

Thump-thump-thump. Her father clomping *up* the basement stairs.

"You really should go," Jackie whispered again, a little louder. "Now!"

The fastest exit was straight ahead through the back yard, over the fence and into the grass verge of a street that ran behind the houses. So off I went, without so much as a goodbye kiss.

And sure enough, behind me as I ran I could hear the *p'twing! p'twing!* of shots from a BB rifle hitting the wooden fence as I made my escape. Thankfully none of them landed in my ass.

Later, Jackie said her father claimed he thought there was a rabbit in his garden. Yeah, right. Who's he, Farmer McGregor?

Needless to say, sadly that was the end of that little romance. Too bad. We liked each other. She was a sweet girl. And remarkably unmessed-up, considering how her father was. But neither of us was willing to take the risk. So we ended it. I've often wondered what became of Jackie. I hope she's OK. And well away from her father.

So with that in mind, did Cassie's father take Gray's chat

with his daughter – for surely her mother would have reported it to him – as overly flirty, maybe even an inappropriate sexual advance? I certainly didn't see it that way. I saw it as entirely innocent. Basic friendliness, even just some musical encouragement.

But then I'm not her father. And even if I were, I certainly wouldn't be as overprotective as he seems to be. Overbearing mother, overprotective father – it's a wonder Cassie isn't completely messed up in her social skills. Then again, maybe she is. Jackie wasn't, but who knows with Cassie? I sure don't. I hardly know her.

Dip. Pull. Wrist.

Dip. Pull. Wrist.

I reached the little boat ramp where I put in and take out the kayak. I felt just pleasantly tired enough from the physical exertion. The mental gymnastics left me more tired than that. Had all this thinking gotten me anywhere? Maybe not. Certainly not anywhere definitive. I was still, as my friend Bill Garner would put it, in a state of articulate confusion.

Better than nothing, I guess.

Chapter 36

I will thank thee, for thou hast heard me.

– Ps. 118, v. 21

Having got home, showered, shaved and changed back into regular clothes. I made myself a fresh pot of tea. The shower helped, but I still needed to warm up from the cold lake.

I checked some papers online. Despite Gray's growing international reputation, only a few even mentioned the death of the promising young countertenor. Those that did, and only briefly, were in England and Europe, where they take early music more seriously and treat countertenors with greater respect. A couple of early music blogs had picked up on Sandra's story – the countertenor network is small but loyal – but to the wider world this was barely a blip.

Sic transit gloria mundi. Thus fades the glory of the world away.

I wanted to talk to Sandra. Running things over in my mind – and occasionally muttering to myself out on the water where no one could hear me – was all very well and good. But I needed someone – a real person – to bounce my ideas off, point out any flaws in my line of reasoning. Sandra, being one of the sharpest people I know, has always been a great sounding board, going all the way back to the days when we worked together in the *Gazette* newsroom.

It was Friday. Had she come to the end of her lobster shifts or would she be working late again tonight? In which case she was probably trying to sleep. I wasn't sure what her sked would be. I decided to risk texting her. If she were sleeping, she'd probably have her phone off.

"*hey*," I texted, "*u up?*"

I waited to see if I'd get a response. Nothing for several minutes. Oh well. Then:

Dun-dun.

"*ya cant sleep. too much coffee*," she texted back. "*whats up?*"

"*want even more coffee*?"

"*sure whatthehell. gimme 15*"

I looked at Wolf happily curled up on her blanket under my desk.

"Good girl," I said. She cocked her head at me. "You stay, pup. I'll be back soon."

Wolf sighed and put her head back down on her paws. It's a dog's life.

Maggie's tea is never as good as my own blend. But beggars can't be choosers. Sandra had already scored a twofer booth against the wall again by the time I arrived, still within our 15-minute window. It was even the same booth we'd had this morning. I think. Sherlock would have known for sure. The lunch rush was over and Maggie's had quieted down again. It would ramp up as dinner approached. Students go for the cheap liver-and-onions dinner special. But for now, I didn't feel guilty taking up a table for just tea (me) and coffee (Sandra, of course. Maybe she never sleeps). Besides, we were regulars. Almost family.

"So, whaddaya got?" Sandra took a healthy swig of her coffee. Scowled. Added another half-spoon of sugar.

I took her through my thought process as I'd been able

to lay it out in my own mind from this morning's paddle. When I'd gotten home, I'd made a few notes in one of the reporter's notepads left over from my *Gazette* days. I flipped it open to the right page. She listened without interrupting.

When I'd finished, Sandra took a final gulp of her coffee and caught our server's eye for a refill.

"We seem to have a surfeit of suspects." She grinned at using 'surfeit.' It's one of those words – like 'eschew' or 'plethora' or 'exacerbate' – that as journalists our editors have all but forbidden us to use. Way too fancy for the newspaper crowd.

I was grateful for the 'we.'

"Seems to me the simplest answer is drunk driver," Sandra said. "Least complicated and in some ways easiest to prove – if we can find the driver."

"Helluva big *if*."

"Ya, it is. But cops are pretty good at that kind of thing."

"You mean if someone drove drunk this time they might have done it before."

"Exactly. So there'd be a record. Of the driver or the vehicle or both. Or they might do it again. And cops will catch them next time."

"I dunno," I said. "Not keen on the idea of just waiting around for some idiot to tie one on and get behind the wheel again. For one, it might take too long. And for another, it could be dangerous for someone else. And of course the driver."

My tea was done. I nodded at our server, who came and filled the little stainless-steel pot with more hot water. I left it to steep.

"So you and the police have looked at other recent hit-and-runs –"

"– Going back almost two years, ya," Sandra said. "Nothing that looks like our guy."

"Or gal."

Sandra gave me a sneer. "Or gal."

"And no luck with any new witnesses who might have seen the SUV drive away that night."

"I talked with Kang yesterday," Sandra said. "Nada. And he's promised to keep me updated. Quite aside from the immediate news story, I think I've persuaded the desk to let me work on a larger feature about drunk driving and general road safety. So I've been compiling stats and info. Good for those slow news days in the summer.

Summer? Sheesh! We're still barely into spring. I was never good at writing stories that far ahead. Give me a shorter deadline any old day. One of the things I always liked about a daily newspaper: The sense of constant renewal. You get the paper out and you turn around and do it all again. Only this time better. Like a snake shedding its skin. One of the problems I was having adjusting to the life of a church musician – having to work so far ahead. Which reminded me I need to get in some quality practice time. On *Messiah* as well as all the Palm Sunday and Easter music coming up.

"Oh, I meant to tell you," Sandra said, "in addition to the cops checking garages and bodyshops for our possibly damaged SUV, I made some calls too. I did a story last summer about young kids souping up their cars, so I got to know not only the guys in the local trade but also a bunch of other hobbyists who do their own work. None of them has seen anything either."

"Unless one of them was driving."

"Ya, I guess. But I get the sense these guys are more interested in tinkering than drinking." She smiled at her own unintended near-rhyme. "I think they'd be inclined to come forward with anything they knew. Keeping it secret would make all of them look bad."

I poured some tea into my mug. A little weaker the second time around. But it would do.

Chapter 37

O remember not the sins and offences of my youth.
– Ps. 25, v. 7

"And need I remind you," Sandra said, "Kang and the other cops are gonna treat Gray's death as an accidental hit-and-run unless and until they have any new evidence to the contrary."

"Ya," I said. "They know about the scribbled music score and the addict ex-girlfriend. They've tried to find her but haven't had any luck. But after talking to Don Patterson, I have a feeling they're not taking that very seriously as an option."

"OK, so if not a random drunk or angry ex, who else might have any reason to hurt or even kill Gray?"

I'd already gone over most of this with Sandra. But it was good to talk it through out loud. We often used to do this with a news story too if one or other of us was having trouble getting a handle on it. (My easily distracted mind of course thought of handle/Handel/*Messiah*. I tried to focus.)

"Well," I said, "all three members of the McBride family – mom, dad, daughter – have a bit of motive if you want to be a little paranoid about it."

"Do you really think getting to sing the solos in a small local production of *Messiah* – sorry, Dugan, no offence – is worth attacking someone?"

"No, I don't, really," I said. "And no offence taken. I know we're not exactly the big time. Having Gray Bergdorf as our soloist definitely cranked us up a notch. But even so, it seems a bit of a stretch. We're still pretty small potatoes."

"True. But let's not forget, quite aside from Carla, with any of the McBrides we might not be dealing with an entirely rational person either. From what you've told me, the father seems like a piece of work. The mother too. And given smothering parents like that, who knows what anger and resentment Cassie might have simmering under the surface?"

Sandra took a final swallow of her second cup of coffee. From this session. Plus the two at breakfast just a few hours ago. And who knows how many cups she'd had to help push her through her overnight lobster shift? It's a wonder she wasn't vibrating.

"And trust me, Dugan," she said. "I was an adolescent girl once. We can be pretty messed up. And I was lucky to have good, supportive parents – hell, they let me go to J-school and become a journalist. Instead of something solid, like a doctor or lawyer or engineer. Or a drywaller, for that matter."

I tried to picture Sandra – who tops out at about 5-foot-3 – hefting 4x8 sheets of drywall. You know what? She'd probably make it work.

"So believe me," she said, "you take even your average pubescent girl – with all the angst, confusion, anger and hormones that entails – and you add in some messed-up, oppressive parents? Well, I can tell you – that could turn out to be a volatile mix."

Terrific, I thought. Cassie, she-wolf of Alliston.

"Hey, do you even know if Cassie can drive? Does she have a licence?"

"She's barely turned 16," I said, "Not sure if she's even had time to get one. I haven't seen her drive. And I know at least one time her dad picked her up after a choir practice.

But I'm not sure how long ago that was. Maybe she got her licence in the meantime."

"I might not matter," Sandra said. "Cassie grew up on a farm. And most farm kids I know of have learned to drive when they're really young, even if it's just the family tractor or and old bush truck.

"In any case, not to worry," Sandra said. "Without stepping on Kang's toes I think I can find out. I've got other sources at the cop shop who owe me favors. I'll look into it just so we know."

"Thanks."

"No prob. You can pay for this coffee too. Call it my fee."

Sandra got up and put on her coat.

"Time for you to go home and sleep?"

"I'll try to get in a few hours this afternoon," she said. "One more lobster tonight and then I've got the weekend to turn myself around. I'm back to days on Monday. Thank God."

"Well, sleep tight. And thanks for listening."

"Anytime. Lemme know how your investigation goes. I'll keep you updated from my end."

And with that she was gone.

My investigation? My investigation, such as it was, had so far yielded nothing but a bunch of possibly unconnected 'suspects' to something that might in the end be nothing more than a tragic accident, maybe criminal negligence. And a bunch of questions to which I was barely any closer to finding the answers.

If the police, with all their resources, had no luck so far tracking down Carla Lumeti, there was even less chance

I'd be able to. Ditto with some random unknown driver. So where did that leave me? It left me with the only possible connections with whom I did have a chance to speak – clan McBride.

Maybe it was time for a road trip to Alliston.

Chapter 38

The singers also and dancers shall say
'All my fresh springs are in thee.'

– Ps. 87, v. 7

When Wolf hears the word 'car,' she gets all excited. Strapped safely in the back seat of Sofia the Fiat, she was ready for a road trip. When she saw we were taking the route north out of town, she got even more excited. She knows the land and my little cabin are up that way.

As huskies go, Wolf is not the most vocal. The shepherd in her helps keep that in check. But when she's lonely or excited, the yips and small howls and singing start to come out. And she loves it up in the woods.

Sorry, pup. Not this time.

As I got closer the top end of town, crossing the main east/west highway and rising out of the limestone bowl that holds Grayston, I deked across a sideroad and took a different road going north and a little west, the two-lane blacktop that would take us to Alliston.

It was a nice drive. No snow on the road but patches still in the shadows on the sides. A few trees that got sunlight had the beginnings of buds.

... proud-pied April, dressed in all his trim,
Hath put a spirit of youth in everything ...

Ah, a little Shakespeare for the road.

Not much more than half an hour later we reached Alliston.

And I realized living in Grayston had spoiled me. Gotta say, Alliston has much less to recommend it.

No lake, for one thing. Not even a river to power an old millwheel. There must have been some reason in its history why a town would build up at this spot on the highway, but damned if I could figure out why. It seemed to be just the proverbial 'wide spot on the road.' Maybe it was the crossroads of two much earlier trading routes. But whatever their importance in the past, their worth was long past now.

The main drag – barely more than three blocks long – had retained some nice old architecture, most of it in old brick, some in stone. Darker than Graystone's limestone. Igneous maybe, or sandstone. Not sure. I'm not a rock expert. (More of a classical guy – *ba-dmp-tshh! I'm here all week, folks. Try the veal!*)

There was a solid-looking stone municipal building, which looked like it combined town hall, post office and police station. Maybe a jail built for two. I presume court cases would end up in Grayston. There were a few fine old trees, but they were scattered. Some old stumps showed signs of other trees long since removed. Maybe taken by blight or lightning strike but never replaced. Not enough money in the budget. It was a town in decline.

There were churches of various denominations and flavors. The church writ large has been a strong influence in almost every town and city for a century or more. Less so now. Not necessarily a bad thing IMO – but don't tell my music committee that.

A quick check online before I left had confirmed only one McBride in the phone listings and a further quick search had shown me a location on the map of a small farm on the outskirts of town. I stopped briefly at the closest thing to a city park that Alliston seemed to offer, parked and took Wolf out for a pee. Better on town grass than McBride's. You never know how some people will take to dogs. Given Harold McBride's reputed quick temper, I didn't want to risk setting him off.

At this time, mid-afternoon, I figured Cassie was probably still at school, though she might be home soon, unless she had some sort of after-school activity. Soccer maybe. Or chess club, for all I know. I was hoping at least Harold would be there, working around the farm or in his repair shop. Mrs. McBride? Who knows? I purposely hadn't called ahead. If people are going to lie to you, best not give them time to prepare.

Maybe none of them would be home and this whole trip would be a waste of my time. Well, it was my time to waste. At least Sofia got a bit of highway time instead of her usual in-town stop-and-go or just sitting in the Grandview's underground garage.

The McBride farm hardly deserved the name. From the fence lines – a mix of old cedar snake rail and slightly newer but also worn post-and-wire – the property covered no more than five acres, maybe less. A frame house, faded white with chipped paint, sat behind a front field that struggled to grow anything. A long, straight dirt lane barely wide enough for one vehicle led from the main road to a small turnaround in front of the house. The centre of the turnaround showed signs of a small garden that might re-emerge in the spring, though it would be a struggle. An attempt – by Mrs. McBride, I imagine – to add a touch of beauty to an otherwise bleak setting.

An open driveshed beside the house stood empty of any vehicles. That probably meant Mrs. McBride was still off somewhere. I could see a sorry-looking barn behind the house where I imagine Farmer McBride kept his few animals – including, I assume, the infamous pig. I wonder if he's still intact? To my right sat a small outbuilding with an open double door and a shed roof. A faded sign said: 'McBride's Small Engine Repair: If It's Broke, We Can Fix It.'

Beside the shed and spilling into the field were a few old cars and a tractor in various states of repair, disrepair and disassembly. Maybe McBride cannibalized the cars for parts. There were also three older SUVs – one a faded black, one battleship grey and one a faded cherry red. Could one of them have hit Gray? Two had front-end damage, one with a cracked tail light, maybe waiting for McBride to repair them. It was not clear to my inexpert eye whether either of them was actually roadworthy. The red one was barely a shell. Maybe it fed parts to the other two.

I parked Sofia on the far side of the turnaround so as not to block the driveshed and got out. Wolf was snoozing in the back seat, so I was happy to leave her there with the windows half-open.

Chapter 39

Thou hast made him but little lower than the angels.

– Ps. 8, v. 5

Someone I had to assume was Harold McBride was in the workshop hunched over an old chainsaw clamped in a vise on a workbench. Pliers, wrenches, hammers and other old tools hung on a large pegboard above the bench. The shop itself held a jumbled assortment of lawnmowers, other chainsaws and at least one snowblower. An old three-wheeled ATV – banned but grandfathered – sat in one corner. Beside it was a snowmobile partly assembled – or partly disassembled, hard to tell.

McBride, intent on sharpening the chainsaw teeth with a small round file, didn't hear me enter. After a moment I cleared my throat and he looked up.

"Help ya?" he said.

"Mr. McBride?"

"Yup."

Terse. Great. At this rate, I'd be here all day.

"I'm Dugan Heywood," I said, extending my hand. "I'm the choir director in Grayston. Your daughter will be singing with us."

McBride put down the file and began to extend his right hand to shake mine. But looking down, he saw it was covered in grease and pulled it back. He took a rag out of his back pocket and wiped his hands. I'm not sure it did much to clean them.

"Sorry 'bout that," he said with half a smile. "Hazard of the job. Dirty fingernails too. The wife hates 'em."

I returned the other half of his smile. No hard feelings.

"Cassie not givin' you any trouble, is she?" he said. "I try to keep her in line but that girl can be wild sometimes."

Really? I thought. I've only met her at a few rehearsals but she's always seemed well-behaved to me. Quiet, shy, keeps to herself. Maybe a little insecure. Hasn't struck me as a wild teen. Knows her notes. And actually looks at the conductor! In my books that makes her just a little lower than the angels.

"No, nothing like that, Mr. McBride," I said. "Cassie's a fine addition to the choir."

"So what brings ya out here, then?"

Clearly, McBride was not one for social calls. He was wearing bib overalls. He took out a small flask out of one of the front pockets and took a long swig. By the look of him not his first of the day. From the smell it might have been bourbon but, not being a drinker myself, I'm not very good at identifying alcohol. Pretty sure it wasn't lemonade. He half-heartedly waved it in my direction but I declined with a smile and a small shake of my head. He looked relieved. And took another swig, shorter this time.

And what *did* bring me out here? I couldn't really come right out and accuse him of murder. For one thing, I had no evidence beyond my own speculation. And for another, his wall of tools was filled with any number of sharp and potentially menacing implements. No point making him angry.

On the other hand, I'd come all this way. And I really did want answers if there were any to be found. Might as well press ahead. McBride came out of the workshop and ambled slowly toward the house with the barn behind. I hope he wasn't leading me back there to help him castrate a pig.

By this time Wolf had woken up and was sitting upright in the back seat, ears perked up, nose twitching, quiet but alert to all the farmland sounds and smells around her.

"You got a dog?" McBride said. "You keep that dog locked up in your little car there, Heywood. I don't want him going after any of my livestock."

I thought of correcting McBride on Wolf's pronouns, but given his hostile mood thought better of it.

"My dog's safe in the car," I said. "Don't worry about it."

"Had a dog once," he said. "Useless thing. No good for hunting. Had to get rid of it." I was afraid to ask what he meant by that. Probably best for me not to know.

McBride turned away from the dog and back to me. "So why are ya here anyway?"

An excellent question. I decided to just forge ahead.

"Well, sir –" might as well be polite "– I'm sure you've heard we had a tragic accident last week. One of my singers was hit by a car. He died later in hospital."

"Ya, the wife mentioned something about that," he said. "Sorry for your loss, I guess. Makes no nevermind to me."

Whatever had brought McBride outside, I guess he'd changed his mind. He took another swig from his flask, turned and headed back toward his shop. I closed the distance between us to keep pace.

"I was just wondering if you or your wife, or maybe Cassie, knew anything about it?" I said. It was a weak card, but the only one I could think of playing. Maybe the booze would loosen his tongue.

"Why would we?"

He had me there.

"I just thought maybe you'd heard something."

"Can't say as I have," he said. "I guess you could ask the wife. She should be back soon."

"And Cassie? I guess she'll be home soon from school."

McBride gave me a look that would put Medusa to shame. Now I know how scared Cassie's date must have felt.

"I'll thank you to leave my daughter alone," he said. "I don't like her talking to strangers."

I thought of pointing out I'm not exactly a stranger. But I figured he wouldn't listen. I thought I'd better not press my luck.

I was going to leave, if not exactly run away, when I heard the sound of a car coming down the lane. McBride heard it too and turned to look.

Within moments, Margaret McBride arrived, driving a medium-sized four-door family sedan in a sort of light bronze color that was no longer in fashion. So it would seem the family car was an old sedan, not an SUV. She put the car in the driveshed, got out and came to us.

"Mr. Heywood," she said, forcing a smile. "How unexpected."

She turned to her husband.

"Harold, how long has Mr. Heywood been here and you haven't even offered him anything? Honestly, there's no hope for you!"

She turned back to me.

"Mr. Heywood, I'm so sorry," she said, taking command. "Harold has no manners. Please, come in the house where it's warm. May I offer you coffee or tea? Something stronger? Harold, you can go back to your tinkering."

Chapter 40

But they are all gone out of the way;
They are altogether become abominable.
There is also none that doeth good, no not one.

– Ps. 14, v. 4

Like the town of Alliston and the rest of the McBride farm, the farmhouse too had seen better days. The kitchen looked like something straight from the Sears catalogue, 1940-ish. Margaret McBride sat me down at an old kitchen table – Formica top, metal-edged trim – and began filling the kettle.

"Just water would be fine, thanks," I said. "I don't want to be any trouble."

"Well, fine. Suit yourself." She drew some water from the kitchen tap and handed me the glass, making it somehow clear that I had insulted her as a hostess.

I was already off on the wrong foot. Time to turn on the charm.

From the kitchen I could see into part of the front room – living room? sitting room? parlor? not sure what to call it. Faded wallpaper and likewise faded furniture. But despite the age, everything seemed well cared for. The McBrides may not be rich, but Mrs. McBride, at least, seemed to take some pride and effort in keeping up appearances.

When in doubt, resort to flattery.

"Your house is charming, Mrs. McBride," I said. "It's so nice to see you've preserved many of the original elements."

"Harrumph!" she snorted. "I do try my best, considering what I've got to work with."

She busied herself at the sink, tidying up things that

didn't look like they needed tidying. She was having trouble keeping still.

"Harold inherited the family farm when his parents passed," she said. "First his father, then his mother. We've been struggling with it ever since."

She wiped her hands on a dish towel and made a move to sit down at the table. But quickly got up again and returned her attention to tidying around the sink – one of those old steel jobs covered in porcelain. Chips and cracks showed signs of its age.

"Take this old kitchen, for instance," she said. "You may call it charming. I call it worn out and barely workable."

She wet a dishrag and wiped the counter for the third time.

"I've been after Harold for years to let me upgrade it – though Lord knows how we'd afford it. Harold's good with those machines, God bless him. When he can stay sober enough to fix anything. But he doesn't bring in much business. I have to do most of it with my bookkeeping around town.

"And of course," she said proudly, "I do have some piano students."

I looked over and saw a worn old upright in the front room.

"Thank God at least Harold can keep our old car on the road," she said. "Which is more than I can say about most of those heaps out in the field."

Mrs. McBride stopped herself, mindful that perhaps she'd revealed a family secret. Or shame. Harold McBride obviously liked his liquor. Was he also the type to liquor up and get behind the wheel? I decided to press on.

"Mrs. McBride," I said, "you may wonder why I'm here.

You know, of course, that Grayston Bergdorf was in a terrible accident."

It was a calculated move for me to call it an accident. No point rousing any suspicion.

"Yes, I heard," she said vaguely, looking up and away from me, as if she'd spotted a smudge near the ceiling. "In fact, I presume that's why you're here. You want Cassandra to be your soloist after all. I'm glad you've come to the right choice. I knew you'd come around eventually."

She sat down again at the table.

"Why," she said, "just the other day I was saying to my Harold that you – being a church man – must have a good heart after all. He didn't believe me, but I have faith. I'm glad you've come to apologize."

Well, this was awkward.

"Actually, Mrs. McBride," I said, stalling for time. "Christine and I haven't really had a chance to discuss what we'll do about the alto solos."

She gave me a cool look.

"Or indeed" I added quickly, "what we're going to do about the production as a whole. We're still undecided."

This did not sit well with Mrs. McBride. But she forced a polite smile.

Struggling to get back on track, I tried the same tack as I had with her husband.

"I know you couldn't have seen anything," I said, "since of course you weren't there. But I wonder since then if maybe you've heard anything?"

Grasping at straws – that's me.

"Mr. Heywood," she said sternly, "I know I'm supposed to feel sorry that he's been in an accident. And I suppose I am.

I am certainly sorry the poor man died. I mean, I wouldn't wish death on anyone."

I nodded sympathetically.

"But I suppose it's no secret that I didn't much care for him," she said. "If it weren't for that abomina–"

She caught herself quickly.

"– If it weren't for that *man* swanning in at the last minute, you should certainly have given the contralto solos to my Cassie."

I held my tongue. Sometimes it's one of my better moves. Not always easy. Don't open that can of worms.

"But have you heard anything that might lead us to whoever was driving that night?"

"I'm sure I haven't," she said tersely. "And I'm sure that's something you should be leaving to the police in any case. I don't know why you're asking me all these questions."

It was really only one question. But why bother to make the point?

"Now, Mr. Heywood," she said, standing, taking my arm and all but lifting me out of my seat, "it's time for you to go. I have to start making Harold his dinner. And Cassandra will be home soon from her singing lesson with *Ms.* Tanaka. And I'd like you gone before she gets here. She's upset enough already, poor girl, having someone she knows die in such a manner. And I won't have you upset her any further."

"I certainly wouldn't want to upset Cassie," I said sincerely. "Thank you for the glass of water."

"You're welcome, I'm sure," she said without any conviction, giving me the bum's rush out the door.

Well at least Wolf was happy to see me. I started up the Fiat and drove carefully down the narrow lane toward the main road. As I got near the road, I saw Cassie turn in on her bicycle.

Poor Cassie. Still too cold to be riding a bike.

Chapter 41

Yet is their pride but labour and sorrow:
so soon passeth it away, and we are gone.

– Ps. 90, v. 11

It's funny how you can put so much effort into something – spending weeks or even months preparing and going over every detail – all for it to be over in what seems like mere moments. When I was a reporter I wasn't much for the long haul – I was more of a quick hit guy, slamming out an overnight theatre or concert review or the fast turnaround on a breaking news story. But I did write a few bigger features that would take weeks of work researching, writing, doublechecking and polishing.

And of course the Gascoyne scandal had both – months of digging and preliminary investigation, the big splash on the Saturday front and several inside pages followed later by a bunch of shorter news hits as the story broke open and worked its way through the court system over the course of several months. I wasn't the only reporter or editor working the story – in fact my part was relatively small. But still, definitely the biggest story I've ever had a hand in.

And now I've learned the life of a church musician is not much different in that regard. All those weeks and months the choir spent preparing the music for Palm Sunday and then Easter and – poof! – now it was done. I hope the congregation appreciated all our efforts.

In fact I'd been so busy with music in the past few weeks that I'd given little thought to Gray Bergdorf and the mystery of the unknown driver. Not that there was much more to think about. The police had no new leads on either the vehicle or whoever was driving it that night. Nor were they any closer to tracking down Gray's mysterious ex-girlfriend.

Marcie – still obviously upset and dealing bravely with her loss – had decided that being useful might help her cope. So she'd put some effort into trying to find Carla, asking some of Gray's old friends from that time. But many of them, being also struggling musicians, had moved on, looking for other work, or were on tour somewhere and hard to track down. So she'd had no luck finding Carla Lumeti. At one point, she told me, she had a line on someone who knew Carla, but that petered out to a dead end.

I'd put a call in to Sandra Novak to see if she'd fared any better.

"No," she said. "Sorry. I figured I'd start with Alliston since maybe there's a connection to the other church choir. I know it's a stretch. But Alliston doesn't have a local newspaper anymore so I asked a friend at the *Repeater* to check it out from her end too. Nothing."

I knew Sandra meant the *Reporter & Times*, once another small independent newspaper in a town about 100 miles north of Grayston – so it might have Alliston in its catchment area. Blackwell had of course also swallowed up that one too. One big happy family.

Given either by journalists against their rivals or by readers themselves, most newspapers have a funny and often snarky nickname. Chosen with at least some affection, I hope. So the *Reporter & Times* becomes *Repeater & Crimes*. Or just *Rip & Tear*. The *Morning Mail* becomes the *Moan & Wail*. Even the big boys get one: *The New York Crimes* (also

L.A. Crimes). The *Washington Pissed. New York Stun.* And of course the *Grayston Gaze At.*

So despite her skills and the resources of the paper – even of another paper in the chain in our area – so far Sandra had struck out on Carla and on the SUV and driver. Damn SUVs are so plentiful it's like looking for a needle in stack of needles. Regardless of make or model, so many of them look pretty much the same. And so many of them have paint on the darker end of the spectrum. I thought again of Leonard Cohen and his final studio album before his death, *You Want It Darker*. And I thought capitalism was supposed to foster innovation and choice? It felt a bit like that old Henry Ford remark about his Model T: "They can have any color they want, so long as it's black."

Easter behind us, we had more time to devote to our big concert, and resumed our rehearsals in earnest. Christine and I had agreed we could leave Sunday's music to the short rehearsal before the Sunday morning service, leaving us free to devote an entire Thursday evening to the good Herr Handel. (Handel lived the last half of his life, about 36 years, in London yet never completely lost his thick Saxon German accent. When he wasn't off travelling – like to Dublin to debut *Messiah* – Handel spent the whole time in a little house at 25 Brook St. Some 200 years later, another great musician – rock guitarist Jimi Hendrix – lived next door, at #23. Together, they're now the Handel & Hendrix Museum. One of these days I'll make it there for a visit.)

The Alliston choir once again trooped onto their rattletrap schoolbus to join us at St. Quentin's. I felt a bit guilty that my choir hadn't yet returned the favor by going to them. But my choir was bigger and posed a bigger logistical challenge. Besides, we'd be going to Alliston next time. Meantime, there was money in my budget to help pay for their gas and bus rental.

I was pleased to see Cassie get off the bus with the others. Even more pleased to see no sign of the formidable Margaret McBride. Nor the belligerent Mr. either. I was hoping that would let me speak with Cassie for a few moments on her own.

Chapter 42

Hearken, O daughter, consider, and incline thine ear;
forget also thine own people and thy father's house.
– Ps. 45, v. 10

I got my chance at the break while the singers were scarfing down cookies and juice. Cassie was off in a corner by herself, looking over her music. She was sitting on one of those chairs with the metal frame and the curved plywood seat and back that you seem to find in every church hall or basement and every school gym. I wish I owned a share of that company. Coulda retired decades ago.

Not wishing to startle her, I strolled over trying to act casual. Not sure she bought it. She looked up suddenly, her defences raised, when she felt me near.

"Hey, Cassie," I said as gently as I could. This was a girl who seemed suddenly alert. Maybe having an alcoholic father keeps you always on edge. She seemed to relax a bit when she saw it was me.

"Oh hi, Mr. Heywood," she said. "I was just looking over some of those runs. Why are they so tricky?"

"Handel liked to show off sometimes, I think."

That earned me a small smile. Progress.

"I was sorry to hear about that singer," she said, opening a line of conversation and saving me the trouble. "He seemed nice. And he had an amazing voice!"

"Have you ever heard a countertenor before?"

"No," she said. "It seemed a bit weird at first – am I allowed to say that? – but once I got used to it, I kinda thought it was impressive. And he was nice enough to talk to me. Told me I had a good voice and I should keep singing."

"That was nice of him."

"Ya," she said, "but my mom didn't like that at all. She nearly went apeshi–" Cassie stopped short. "My mother wasn't pleased that he was talking to me."

"Why's that, do you think?"

"I dunno," Cassie said, casting her eyes down. "My parents don't like me talking to boys. My dad especially. He's even worse than my mom. But it's not fair! I'm 16 now! I'm old enough to be dating boys. But they hardly let me."

I thought back to my high school girlfriend Jackie when we were 15. And her angry father with the rifle. And Cassie's father with the pig and his big knife. But poor Cassie's social life – or lack thereof – was undoubtedly a distraction. If I was going to get any answers and help bring Gray's killer to justice, I needed to get this conversation back on track.

"Hey Cassie," I said, trying again to be casual and non-confrontational, "have you heard anything about what happened that night?"

Not my most subtle segue, but I was mindful that rehearsal would start again soon and we didn't have much time to talk.

"No, I don't know anything about that," she said quickly. "Why would I? I wasn't there."

She was echoing what her father had said. And she seemed suddenly wary again. I wondered why.

"Oh, no reason," I said. "One of your other choir members was there and I wondered if she'd said anything."

It was a weak line of questioning – and I knew it even as it was coming out of my mouth. But I didn't know what else to say. I was just trying to keep Cassie talking in case she said anything useful.

"No, she didn't," Cassie said. And with eminent logic, added, "You should just ask her."

Well, I couldn't argue with that. So far, my grand journalist investigative skills had gotten me precisely nowhere. And I was running out of ideas.

I was hoping to tease more information out of her – not that I was sure how to do that – when someone noticed our 10 minutes was up and made their impressive whistle again.

It was time to go back into the sanctuary to rehearse.

Cassie stood up, clutching her music in front of her like it was a baby. Turning to me, she said "I'm sorry I couldn't be more help, Mr. Heywood."

Yup, I thought. You and be both, kid. You and me both.

Chapter 43

Keep me, O Lord, from the hands of the ungodly:
preserve me from the wicked men
who are purposed to overthrow my goings.

– Ps. 140, v. 4

As usual, I was the last to leave the church. Christine got her Alliston folks safely back onto their trusty schoolbus and headed back home. My choristers left in dribs and drabs, some to their cars, some to walk home, the university kids back to their dorms or shared apartments in the student ghetto.

I closed up the piano and put on its cover. I stacked up a few stray chairs and headed for the door, turning off lights as I went. After one final look, I flicked down the last light switch, went out the door, locked it behind me and started walking down the street toward the Grandview. Wolf would be waiting for me to take her for her final walk of the night before bed.

A light rain had started again. More of my old gran's Scotch mist – just enough to scatter the light and darken the sky. And to have made the roads and sidewalks a little slick. I was glad my shoes had rubber soles for the traction but wished I'd had the foresight to wear my rubber boots. Ah well, it was only about four blocks to home. I was walking on the west sidewalk, with the city park to my right. I looked over but didn't see anyone walking their dog. Too bad. Wolf would have no one to say hi to.

I was nearing the corner by the last gaslamp when I became aware of a car coming up behind me. I'd probably heard the engine before fully registering it in my brain. As I turned to look, the car sped up and seemed to be headed straight for me – though not in a straight line. Even in the narrow old street, it was weaving wildly.

For a moment I had a horrible thought that this might be the same vehicle and driver that had hit Gray Bergdorf. Coincidence? Or connection?

C'mon, Dugan, I told myself, *don't be paranoid!*

Besides, as it got closer, I could it wasn't an SUV anyway, just a regular old car. And clearly not black, but some lighter color.

But despite all its weaving, it was still coming right at me. And gaining speed.

In one of those moments when they say your life might flash before your eyes, with a bump and a lurch the car mounted the curb of the sidewalk right behind me. I had to jump out of the way to avoid getting hit. I landed with a *thump* on the ground, grateful for the grass in the park. Also grateful we have a conscientious poop-and-scoop dog community. At least grass stains might be the worst I'd have to worry about.

As I picked myself up, wet but alive and with no bones broken, I could see the car speeding off. I couldn't be sure, but it looked like a man behind the wheel. Just as it turned the corner, it passed under the gaslamp. Maybe it was a trick of the firelight, but it looked to me like the car had a bit of a bronze tint.

I rushed home and put in a call to Kang, glad he'd given me his card with a direct line. Straight to voicemail, so I left him a brief message. Told him what had just happened and what

I suspected. Suggested he'd probably want to talk to Harold McBride. Asked him to call me when he got this message.

Next I texted Sandra.

"hey meet me 4 brkfst @7. possible scoop TK"

No immediate reply. Maybe she was already asleep.

I figured it was safe enough to take Wolf back to the park for her walk. The murderous car was probably gone back where it came from. And I'm pretty sure I know where that is. Still, I kept my eyes peeled for any vehicles, especially any family sedans the color of a '70s fridge. Harvest Gold, the carmaker probably called it. Or Bronze Sunset. I knew someone once whose car color was Tahitian Rose. Well, easy for him to find it in a parking lot.

Nevertheless, just to be safe, I kept Wolf on the leash and headed for the middle of the park, safely away from any streets or vehicle access. Once again we had the whole place to ourselves. That's the thing about rain: It keeps away all but the stalwarts.

Wolf wasn't too keen either, so she wrapped up her business quickly. As I picked up the result, she was doing that thing, kicking back with her hind legs. Stretching or whatever. Some people think it's instinctive, to cover up their poop with leaves, dirt or whatever else is lying around. Makes sense, I guess. But I have no idea if that's really true. Dog behavior is sometimes a mystery. And I think we often attribute human characteristics to them that don't necessarily apply. Wolf looked at me and gave a gentle tug on her halter. I guess we're headed home. I dropped the poop bag in the organics bin as we passed by.

When we got home there was a single reply text from

Sandra:

"k"

Kids these days: Too lazy even to write "OK."

Chapter 44

O let the wickedness of the ungodly come to an end,
but guide thou the just.

– Ps. 7, v. 9

Our breakfasts came and Sandra tucked right in. She was already working on her second mug of coffee. I was only halfway through my first mug of tea. I'd already filled her in with a brief rundown – pardon the pun – of the events from last night.

"So after I got your text last night I called Kang first thing this morning," she said. "I know his shift usually starts at 6."

"Keener!" I said, half teasing, half impressed. "So what did he say?"

"He played coy at first," she said. "But once I reminded him we're on the same team, all working toward justice, *blah-blah-blah*, he opened up a bit. Not sure if he really wanted to help or was just tired of me nagging him."

Sandra grinned over the edge of her mug.

"Wear 'em down with persistence, I always say."

I nodded at her and smiled back.

"So anyway," she said, "he told me there'd been a new development – I presume that was your call to him last night – and acting on a tip they had a possible suspect in the case."

"Did he tell you who?"

"Not at first, but I got it out of him."

"Lemme guess," I said. "Negative localizing."

Sandra grinned again. "You betcha. I asked if the suspect was a Grayston resident. He said no. I asked if he knew where the suspect lived. He hemmed and hawed a bit but finally said yes he did.

"So I figured, based on everything you and I have been talking about, I'd take an educated guess. Asked him if the suspect might be someone from Alliston named McBride."

"And?"

"And – off the record, mind you, and not for attribution – he said yes it was."

"So what happens now?"

"Kang went back on the record and said Grayston police had 'reached out' – I love when they lapse into cop-speak – to 'a sheriff in a nearby community' this morning to bring the 'person in question' to Grayston for questioning."

"Why here and not there?" Although I think I knew the answer.

"Well, the hit-and-run against Grayston Bergdorf happened here. And although Kang wouldn't admit on the record that they're likely connected, the near-miss against you last night was here in town too. So really it's all part of Kang's case. And I gather the Alliston sheriff is just as happy to have someone else handle all the process and the paperwork."

Sandra waved at our server – another student, but not the one we'd had last time – for a refill. Expertly trained, she came back with a carafe in each hand. More coffee for Sandra, hot water for my little metal teapot. Can't beat the service at Maggie's. Nor the prices.

"So I've got at least a squib to file online for today," Sandra said. "And with any luck, well before deadline, enough to write a bigger story for the Saturday paper."

"So Kang will be interviewing Harold McBride today?"

"That's the plan," she said.

After I got home, I thought of calling Kang or Don for an update, but decided against it. For one thing, with any luck by now Kang was already deep into questioning Harold McBride about his whereabouts last night and, more important, on the night Gray was struck. And for another, they probably wouldn't talk to me anyway. I'm not with the paper anymore, so it's not like they have any obligation to me professionally. And I didn't want to burn off whatever goodwill I might still have.

Might need that again some other time. Who knows?

So meantime, I had to do that thing journalists hate the most: Wait for further developments.

Best thing to do while waiting? Distract myself. Leaving Wolf safely curled up under my desk, I walked over to the church. Time to put in some effort at the organ.

I'm a big believer in 'two birds with one stone.' For instance, as a singer, I don't much like choir warmups. At least not the ones that are just random little runs or scales or triads. Nor random vowel exercises or chord shifts.

They have a point – I get it – I just find them mostly to be a waste of time and effort. Maybe it's all those years spent ever since I was a boy at having to learn large wodges of music for unrelenting weekly services. Time is short. Time, as the lawyers like to say, is of the essence.

So, say I, why waste it being random? When I took over this choir – more or less by accident – I resolved to make the choir warmups more efficient, if not even more enjoyable. So we warm up on the repertoire we're going to be singing anyway. Hymns and psalm chants are always good fodder. And now, since we're doing it, Handel can show us the way.

You want runs and scales? Heck, *Messiah* is crammed

with them. Need to work on tuning and blending? Pick any bar or two with some interesting chord progressions and work through them super-slowly, paying attention to each subtle change. The opening bars of *Since by Man came Death* (I had a twinge thinking of Gray's mutilated *Messiah* score) are a challenge fit enough for any choir.

When my mind's awhirl and it's not convenient to kayak, the next best thing to bring order to my universe is to sit at the keyboard and play a fugue. They start off deceptively simple and become increasingly intricate. But it's wonderful to see all the melodic threads – the subject, answer, countersubject and development – come together and work their magic. At my skill level, I can manage only the simpler ones by Bach. Or any of his little two- or three-part inventions.

Or in this case – two birds with one stone – the final *Amen* of *Messiah*, a fugue Handel builds on a long, five-bar subject. Different from the bombast of the *Hallelujah* chorus, Handel's final musical triptych – *Worthy Is the Lamb/ Blessing and honor/Amen* – brings *Messiah* to a fitting and noble close.

I played through the *Amen* fugue. So capably constructed, so neat and orderly. In many ways so unlike life. Or death.

Chapter 45

When my father and my mother forsake me,
the Lord taketh me up.

– Ps. 27, v. 12

By the time I got home in the early afternoon, Sandra had already filed an online squib of what she had so far. Which wasn't much beyond the brief hed:

Police make arrest
in hit-and-run death

Her story – only two grafs and carefully non-specific – didn't name the accused but it did say where they were from. Attributed to Kang, it simply said Grayston police, with the help of the Allison sheriff, had arrested and detained an Alliston resident in connection with the injury and later death of a man previously struck by a vehicle on a Grayston street approximately two months ago. Police said they would release further details pending charges.

So that was it. For now, anyway. Like everyone else, I had to wait til Saturday's print edition to get more of the story. And, I have to admit, what I read came as a surprise.

My Saturday morning began like most of my others. Wolf and I went for a walk and then I went for a paddle. The lake was still cold, but I decided since it was now (barely) the merry month of May I should ditch the wetsuit. The water was still plenty cold, but I could manage. And frankly, the wetsuit's bulky and a pain.

When I returned and stowed the kayak in the back yard,

I brought the *Gazette* in from my front door – daily home delivery is still an old-fashioned miracle – had a shower, made myself a pot of tea and sat at the counter with the paper in front of me, ready to dive in.

Nothing on Grayston Bergdorf worthy of the front page. The usual global troubles, a story (continued inside in the City section) about plans to rework some of the one-way streets for "traffic-calming" – oh great, more chaos. And a lighter story as a zipper along the bottom about Mrs. McGillicuddy's lost cat finding its way home. Our longtime readers like the happy ones.

Gray didn't even make the City front – the front and turn were all about the one-way streets, complete with maps and a breakout infographic of the proposed cost. (A lot.)

Sandra's follo story on Gray got only a few inches of one column inside on the third City page. I could tell some of it was a rewrite of the story she'd filed earlier. But it was not quite what I'd expected:

**Police charge
Alliston resident
in hit-and-run death**

After an investigation that included the Alliston sheriff's department, Grayston police have arrested and charged an Alliston resident in connection with the hit-and-run injury and later death of a man on a Grayston street two months ago.

Officer Liu Kang of the Grayston and District Police Department said the driver of the vehicle, during questioning and after speaking with counsel, had made a full confession to police – which, Kang said, "has made our job easier."

Reading from an admitted statement of facts, Kang told the *Gazette* the driver of an SUV had

> struck Grayston Bergdorf, 24, on the street in front of Clancy's bar on Grant Street on March 14 and then driven away, failing to remain at the scene. Bergdorf had been at the bar visiting with friends. Witnesses of the event had helped police identify the vehicle, Kang said, which eventually led investigators to the driver. Bergdorf died in hospital of his injuries shortly after the incident.
>
> Police had sought a charge of involuntary manslaughter. But in a brief court appearance Friday and in a plea deal at the behest of counsel, the driver agreed to plead guilty to a reduced charge. Since this is a first offence, Judge Albert Galway set bail at $10,000 and scheduled a sentencing hearing in two weeks' time.
>
> Charged with negligent driving causing death is Margaret Ann McBride, 44, of 2499 County Road 10, Alliston.

Well, hell. That last graf was a kicker. And here – especially since our little run-in Thursday night – I thought the killer was more likely Harold McBride, not Cassie's mother. Have to admit I'm glad it wasn't Cassie. Nice to know there's still some innocence in this world.

"Whaddaya know, Wolf," I said, "that was not what I expected."

She looked at me and turned her head to one side, cocking one ear as if to better tune in. Can you imagine if our ears could swivel like that? She does that when she doesn't understand what I'm saying to her. Which happens a lot.

I texted Sandra:

"nice story but still so many questions"

A pause, then *dun-dun.*

"thx."

"so?"
"sorry, bub. off having fun. wait 4 mon, will give u deets."
"k"
See? I can be down with the kids. I'm hip to the lingo.

Chapter 46

Thou didst cause thy judgment
to be heard from heaven.

– Ps. 76, v. 8

"Gotta admit, I'm a bit surprised at Margaret McBride's age."

Sandra gave me a dirty look.

"No," I said. "Not from her appearance. From her manner, her behavior, she seems much older. But Cassie's only just 16, so I guess if you do the math, 44 makes more sense."

"Well, Harold's almost 10 years older than his wife," Sandra said, "so that probably threw you off too. And a life of hard drinking will also age you. Or so I'm told. I wouldn't know."

"And I have to say," I said, "much as I didn't care for Mrs. McBride, old Harold was much higher on my suspect list. After meeting him, right at the top. Especially after he tried to run me over last week after choir."

"Nah," said Sandra, peering at me over her coffee cup and taking a swig. "For me it was the crazy ex-girlfriend. The whole time. All that scribbling must have thrown me off."

"Good thing we're not cops."

"Yup. Good thing."

We were once again at Maggie's for our usual Monday morning breakfast. And so once again, all was right with the world. I can't speak for whether God was in in his heaven. Not my department.

But that still left some nagging details and loose ends to

tie up. George Papadakis himself arrived with our breakfast plates, both in one hand – the other had a coffee carafe – and laid them down in front of us.

"There you go, Senators," he said. "More coffee, Ms. Novak?"

Even George knew that was a dumb question. He was just being polite. Force of habit. He filled her mug and then went off to do the same for another customer.

"OK," I said. "So I have questions. Have you got answers?"

"Probably most of them. Shoot."

"Well, for starters," I said, "how was it Margaret that rammed into Gray Bergdorf and not Harold? He's the one with the anger issues. And the drinking problem. And who's obsessed with protecting Cassie."

"All true," Sandra said, "but let's not forget: Margaret is the one with the overweening ambition."

Sandra smiled happily at 'overweening.' Another one of those forbidden $50 words.

"Margaret is your overly pushy stage mother," she said. "Wants her daughter to become a big star. As far as she was concerned, Bergdorf had robbed Cassie of her big chance to shine. So he had to go. Frankly, I'm surprised she didn't take any potshots at you too."

I'd finished my eggs and was savoring my last piece of bacon, nice and crisp. I picked it up and took a bite.

"I'm a little surprised at that myself," I said. "OK, so fill me in on the rest of it."

"Gonna need more coffee," Sandra said, and smiled across the room at George. Not sure, but she might even have batted her eyelashes. They're nice eyelashes.

"Just to get the formalities out of the way," Sandra said, "a lot of this info Kang gave me on deep background and off the record. Not for publication. Or at least not until after sentencing. So of course you won't repeat any of this."

"Of course not," I said. "Scout's honor."

"I know you were never a scout. But I'll hold you to your word anyway."

I nodded just to seal the deal.

"Besides which," Sandra said, "He gave me details because I told Kang I want to do a bigger story on him and the department and the work they do. Not just in solving this case, but others too. For a small town, we have a remarkably high murder rate, you know."

"I know," I said. And tried not to look sheepish.

Chapter 47

The sacrifice of God is a troubled spirit:
a broken and contrite heart,
O God, shalt thou not despise.

– Ps. 51, v. 17

Sandra started in: "When the Alliston sheriff went to the farm early last Friday morning to deliver Harold McBride to Kang in Grayston for questioning, Margaret went along too for moral support. Maybe she was hoping they wouldn't have enough evidence to charge him with anything. After all, they just had your vague description of the car and driver. And she must have also been hoping they wouldn't make any connection to her."

"OK," I said, "so far, so good. But how do we get from there to Margaret blurting out a full confession?"

"Blame guilt, I guess," Sandra said. "Also love."

"Not sure I follow."

"Sure you do," Sandra said. "It makes sense once you know the whole story."

"Fine," I said, gesturing broadly, but careful not to spill any tea from the mug in my hand, "the podium is yours."

It went something like this:

Ambitious for her daughter – and probably living vicariously through her – Margaret McBride was furious when Christine and I passed over Cassie and hired Gray Bergdorf as our alto soloist instead. Bad enough that Cassie didn't get the solos, but Margaret was even more furious that they had gone to a *man*. How dare we?! Margaret also admitted that at one of the rehearsals, she'd stolen Gray's music and written all over it in heavy black marker.

That explained what she'd been doing sitting at the back of the church during that rehearsal. I thought she'd been looking down at her cellphone. No, she was circling and underlining every word like 'die' and 'death' and 'despisèd.' Venting her anger.

So it hadn't been Carla Lumeti after all. Marcie must have thought it was Carla but also that, if he'd noticed it, Gray had just never told her about the markings. Wouldn't want to have worried her.

But taking her vengeance on Gray's music score wasn't enough for Margaret. So when Margaret overheard plans for the singers to gather at a bar the next night, she decided to take things a step farther. She'd taken one of Harold's broken-down SUVs from the field beside his shop – the battleship grey one, as it turned out, was slightly more drivable – and driven down to the bar in Grayston and parked nearby. Maybe she'd planned to confront Gray. Or maybe just sit and stare at him and seethe from the safety of the vehicle.

But when she saw him come out from the bar, something in her head snapped. She fired up the SUV and drove at him.

"Margaret swears she didn't intend even to hit him, let alone kill him," Sandra says. "Just scare him. But I guess a little drinking runs in the family and she admitted she'd taking a bit of liquid courage from a bottle while she'd been sitting there.

"As to how much, who knows?" Sandra said. "But maybe enough to impair both her judgment and her reflexes. Besides, she said, she wasn't used to driving an SUV – it's much bigger than her regular car and the handling's different.

The tires were nearly bald. And with the existing front-end damage, maybe the steering was squiffy too. And she'd forgotten to turn on the headlights. With that and the rain she couldn't see very well. She misjudged her distances."

Sandra drained the last of her coffee.

"Oh, and the reason you couldn't see a licence plate? There wasn't one. And on top of that, the bulb at the back over the plate was burned out. That SUV should never have been on the road."

"Where was Harold in all this?"

"Funny you should ask," Sandra said. "As it turns out, Harold has a solid alibi for the incident involving Gray. He was at his regular weekly Friday poker night with the boys. And he'd taken the family car. Which is why Margaret had to drive the SUV and why Harold – at the time – had no idea she'd done so."

"That still doesn't really get us to a confession from Margaret."

"Patience, Sherlock. All will become clear."

Chapter 48

For lo, thine enemies, O Lord, lo, thine enemies shall perish
and all the workers of wickedness shall be destroyed.

– Ps. 92, v. 9

Since we were going to be here for a while longer, I was thinking of ordering more tea. And maybe some pie. After all, we'd sort of solved another murder case. Worth celebrating.

"Hey, you want pie? I'm buying."

"You're buying the whole breakfast, buddy," Sandra said. "Call it the price of getting this terrific inside scoop."

Fair enough. I flagged down George and ordered us more tea, coffee and two slices of pie. Sandra went for cherry but I stuck with apple. What can I say? I'm a traditionalist. No ice cream, though. Trying to watch my girlish figure.

"Right," Sandra said as the pies arrived, "back to Margaret confessing."

She took a bite of pie and a sip of coffee. I don't think I've ever seen her look happier.

"You have to remember," she said, "the thing with Gray was almost two months ago. More than six weeks, anyway. So Margaret has had that whole time to think about what she did. Worry about it. Let it fester just beneath the surface. Turns out the guilt was killing her. And the fear of being caught. Harold told Kang he knew something was off, but he didn't know what. He'd also noticed that the old grey SUV had moved a bit. And that puzzled him. Margaret hadn't quite put it back in the same place. But since it already had front-end damage from long before, whatever there might have been from hitting Gray – if any – wasn't enough to be noticeable. Maybe subconsciously Margaret had even counted on that.

"So anyway, I think Harold had grown suspicious of something, even if he didn't know what it was. But he'd started to put two and two together."

"And when I came around asking questions and sticking my nose in," I said, "that probably set him off even more."

"Yup," Sandra said. "Harold confronted Margaret about her odd behavior, and about why was this church guy from Grayston asking them all these questions. But of course she couldn't admit to him what she'd done. Instead, she vents some more about Cassie missing out on her big debut and how much she dislikes Gray. Told Harold again about Gray 'flirting' with their daughter – we know he hadn't been, but Margaret played it up for Harold's benefit."

"Probably in her mind that helped justify taking a run at him."

"Exactly," Sandra said. "So now Harold's all worked up and, with Gray out of the picture, he decides to focus all his anger on you, Dugan."

"Gee, lucky me."

"Add a hip flask to a barrel of anger and put it behind the wheel – you're lucky you got out of that encounter unscathed."

Sandra finished the last of her pie and looked at me.

"You still want to know about the confession."

"Yes, I do."

"OK," she said, "here's the deal: The cops had brought Harold in to ask him about trying to run you over the other night. Margaret's in the interview room with him. At this point, Kang told me, it was still just a friendly bunch of questions. Kang's a pretty low-key cop and he didn't see any need yet to play hardball."

"Smart guy."

"Ya. So he's just laying groundwork: 'Do you own a bronze-colored sedan? Where were you on Thursday night? Had you driven to Grayston?' – that sort of thing.

"Harold's feeling cornered," Sandra said, "probably still hungover and with a headache. And maybe his memory's a little fuzzy. Also, he's trying to protect Margaret – from what, he's not quite sure, but maybe he suspects her of something."

"So he's being vague," I said, "and evasive."

"Right," Sandra said. "Meanwhile, Margaret's wallowing in her own guilt. And getting more and more worried that Harold might end up in jail for something. It's not clear to me yet whether she'd figured out what Harold had done to you or whether maybe he told her before going to bed and passing out."

"Or she might have been figuring it out as she sat there listening to the questioning."

"Something like that," Sandra said. "In any case, you've got a husband and wife – who despite their faults do still seem to care about each other. And each of them is trying to cover up for the other. Finally, Mrs. McBride couldn't take the pressure anymore. And it all came tumbling out of her."

"So what happens now?"

"Well, like my story says, Margaret has accepted a plea deal and will face sentencing in a couple of weeks."

"Didn't she get bail?"

"The judge set bail at $10,000," Sandra said. "I don't think the McBrides have that kind of money. Maybe they can get a line of credit on the family farm. Otherwise, I guess she spends some time in jail pending sentencing. Presumably here. Or maybe Alliston. That would make visiting easier for Harold and Cassie."

"Are the cops going to charge Harold?"

"Kang said they won't bother," Sandra said. "Unless you want to make a big federal case about it, they have only your word and a vague description of the car and driver. Once Margaret started blurting out her confession, Harold kinda clammed up about the other thing."

"Probably not worth pressing it," I said.

"Sure," Sandra said. "And besides, Harold was so upset that he made Kang a solemn promise that he'd stop drinking, right then and there. Even handed Kang his hip flask."

"Wow."

"Any other issues you'd like me to resolve for you?" Sandra said.

"Yes, while we're at it," I said. "Did you ever find out whether Cassie has a driver's licence?"

"I did," Sandra said. "And no she doesn't. Not that that necessarily might have stopped her, being a farm girl. But in any case, we know it was Margaret driving the SUV that hit Gray."

"Right. And what's the deal with Carla?"

"Ah, the ex-girlfriend, yes," Sandra said. "Marcie and I have been keeping in touch on that. She was finally able to track down the friend who was letting Carla sleep on her couch."

"And?"

"First off," Sandra said, "we know Carla wasn't the one who defaced the music – that was also Margaret."

"OK."

"But more important, even if Margaret hadn't confessed, we know Carla could not have been the one who ran over Gray. She couldn't even have been the one stalking him here in Grayston."

"How come?"

"Because she's been in rehab since almost a month before the whole Gray thing happened, before he even got here," Sandra said. "Off in the woods somewhere at a special retreat. Basically a self-imposed exile. More like a prison. Or at least a monastery. You swear a commitment to stay in the 90-day program and not leave until it's done. She gets only one phone call per week. The friend says she's been sticking with it."

"Good," I said. "Let's hope it takes."

Chapter 49

Sing unto the Lord a new song:
sing praises lustily with a good courage.

– Ps. 33, v. 3

After just a few more rehearsals, we took to the stage. Our *Messiah* performances – first in Grayston at St. Quentin's, then a runout the next night in Alliston at St. Andrew's – were a big success. Financially – which would help the funding of both our choirs – but more important to me, artistically. The singers and the band did a fine job. And even better, they all seemed to be enjoying themselves. And each other.

Yes, of course it's nice to get all the notes right – or even most of them – and to interpret and present the music with nuance and integrity. And to the best of their ability, our musicians did just that. Which is great. And something to be proud of, especially for an amateur group.

But I was also proud of the fact that everyone had poured their hearts and souls into not just producing the notes but into really bringing the music alive. For me, that's about as close as I get to a true religious experience. And that's good enough for me.

With the loss of Grayston Bergdorf, we had to make some changes. Thankfully, my alto section lead, Meg, was available after all to sing some solos. She did a lovely job with the big alto aria near the start of Part II, the poignant and heartfelt *He was despisèd* – which in any case Handel wrote for that first performance in Dublin specifically for a contralto, not one of two countertenor soloists. So that even felt historically authentic.

Out of respect for Gray, we dropped *But who may abide*?/ *Refiner's fire* from the program. I felt the loss, but I'm not sure most of the audience knew the difference. Our bass soloist, Gerry, admitted he'd never sung it and barely knew it. So that was a non-starter. And besides, I'll admit the countertenor in me could never – *ahem* – abide a bass singing it. Under the circumstances, I felt no one else but Gray could have done it justice. Best leave it be.

After the final performance in Alliston – as we all gathered over coffee, juice and homemade goodies in their church basement – I had a few moments to speak with Cassie McBride. I told her I was glad she'd stuck with us to sing.

"Thanks, Mr. Heywood," she said softly. "It's what my mom would have wanted. I didn't want to let her down."

"I'm sorry she couldn't be here to hear you sing," I said.

"Ya," Cassie said. She sounded tired, but whether from singing or sadness I wasn't sure. Probably both.

"Someone from the choir made a recording tonight," she said. "I'll be able to take that to Mom the next time I get to visit her."

"Well, I hope you stick with your singing," I said. I didn't know what else to say.

"I probably will," she said. "But it was always my mom who wanted me to become a big star, not really me. From what Grayston Bergdorf said, I don't think I'd like spending all that time away from home, living in hotel and motel rooms. Doesn't sound like fun."

"I'm with you on that," I said. "And by the way, are you still at home? How's your father doing?"

"He's OK, thanks for asking. He's been going regularly

to AA meetings and next week he's checked himself into a rehab place for at least a month. You know, I tried to warn my mother about his drinking and his temper. But she wouldn't listen. I think she was in denial too."

Mature words coming from a young girl. Maybe Cassie was getting some therapy too, even if only from her school guidance counsellor. Good for her.

"So when Dad goes away," she said, "I'll be living in town with my aunt, my mom's sister. Which is good, 'cause it's closer to school, so a shorter bike ride. I don't think I want to get my driving licence anytime soon."

-30-

About the author

David W. Barber is a longtime newspaper journalist, musician, composer and the internationally bestselling author of *Bach, Beethoven and the Boys; Getting a Handel on Messiah; Bach, Beethoven and the Grrrls; Bach, Beethoven for Kids* and nearly a score of other books of humorous classical music history and literature, including the speculative fiction collection *Atonement and other stories*. *Hotshot* is his third Dugan Heywood mystery novel, following on the heels of *Hedshot* and *Mugshot*. In a varied career, among David's more interesting jobs have been short stints as a roadie for Pope John Paul II, a publicist for Prince Rainier of Monaco and a backup singer for Avril Lavigne. He learned (though not very successfully) transcendental meditation from the same maharishi who taught The Beatles.

Learn about his other books at IndentPublishing.com

Read his blog at DavidWBarber.com

Find his music at SheetMusicDirect.com
and SheetMusicPlus.com

Books by David W. Barber
with illustrations by Dave Donald
Available in print and/or as ebooks
from Indent Publishing

A Musician's Dictionary
(1983)
(Revised and expanded in 2011 as
Accidentals on Purpose: A Musician's Dictionary)

Bach, Beethoven and the Boys:
Music History as It Ought to Be Taught
(1986, 35th-anniversary edition revised 2021)

When the Fat Lady Sings:
Opera History as It Ought to Be Taught
(1990, 35th-anniversary edition revised 2025)

If It Ain't Baroque:
More Music History as It Ought to Be Taught
(1992, 30th-anniversary edition revised 2022)

Getting a Handel on Messiah
(1995, 30th-anniversary edition revised 2025)

Tutus, Tights and Tiptoes:
Ballet History as It Ought to Be Taught
(2000, revised edition 2023)

Bach, Beethoven Going Baroque:
Even More History as It Ought to Be Taught
(2023)

Bach, Beethoven and the Grrrls:
Women's Music History as It Ought to Be Taught
(2024)

Other Books by David W. Barber
Available in print and/or as ebooks
from Indent Publishing

The Last Laugh:
Essays and Oddities in the News
(2000)

Quotable Alice
(2001)

Quotable Sherlock
(2001)

Quotable Twain
(2002)

The Adventure of the Sunken Parsley:
and Other Stories of Sherlock Holmes
(2011)

Better Than it Sounds:
The Music Lover's Quotation Book
(2013)

Think Again!
by Leo Tolstoy, with annotations and commentary
by David W. Barber
(2022)

Atonement and other stories
(2022)

Leacock Laughter
(2023)

Dugan Heywood Mysteries
Hedshot (2023) / *Mugshot* (2024) / Hotshot (2025)

Other Books by
Indent Publishing

Available in print and/or as ebooks
from Indent Publishing

Learn to Play
by Susie Beghin
(2022)

A Feast of Wolves
by Wilson Coneybeare
(2022)

Wild Strawberries Along the Mackenzie
by Bernard R. Blishen
(2023)

Learn to Play Too
by Susie Beghin
(2024)

Stop Selling Real Estate & Start Helping People
by Matilda Nestoroska
(2024)

Find all Indent books at our website:
IndentPublishing.com

Manufactured by Amazon.ca
Acheson, AB

31978305R00125